<u>A NOVEL</u>

KASEY LAINE

Dionndra Reneé

MANCHU ESTATE LLC / NEW YORK

Dionndra Reneé / Manchu Estate LLC
3646 Harper Ave
Bronx, New York 10466
www.manchuestate.com

Publisher's Note: This is a work of fiction. Names, characters, places, and incidents are a product of the author's imagination. Locales and public names are sometimes used for atmospheric purposes. Any resemblance to actual people, living or dead, or to businesses, companies, events, institutions, or locales is completely coincidental.

Book Layout © 2014 BookDesignTemplates.com

Kasey Laine/ Dionndra Reneé. -- 1st ed.
ISBN 978-1-7329208-0-4 paperback

ISBN 978-1-7329208-1-1 e-book

This book is dedicated to my parents,
Frank and Charlene

For encouraging me to chase my dreams and
believing they could actually come true.
Oh, and that little thing called unconditional love,
thanks for that too.
Love you

Dionndra Reneé

Behind every young child who believes in himself
is a parent who believed first.

Matthew L Jacobson

KASEY LAINE

CONTENTS

Chapter One:

An Innocent Teenager

O n this night, everything changed. The only thing that separates adventure and danger is a fine line. Tonight, that line has been crossed. As a teenager, school dances and the latest teen stars are the topics of every conversation. The most important moments of a teenager's social life happens on the weekend. A seemingly normal night slowly unravels at the seams.

"Let's get out of here." Riley walks over to her dresser to get a pair of pants. As the vivacious and outgoing one in the group, she is anxious to start her evening with her two best friends. She loves spending weekends with them at their favorite place, the movie theater. She quickly puts her pants on.

Julia, a flighty soul, follows behind. She changes into one of Riley's shirts; wearing Riley's clothes on their outings has become a usual thing for her. She is always quick to appease Riley, who is a lot more assertive than she is. Comfortable in their skin, Julia and Riley show little concern about changing in front of each other. Tracie, on the other hand, is painstakingly shy and private. Even in front of her two closest friends, she is extremely modest. While Riley and Julia change clothes, she slips away undetected. She grabs her shirt out of her overnight bag and walks into the bathroom to change.

Julia and Riley sit on the bed, waiting for Tracie to come out of the bathroom. While they wait, Riley holds her hand out to check her nail polish. Julia looks into a compact mirror and applies bright lipstick to her thin lips.

When Tracie exits the bathroom, Riley and Julia acknowledge her with a smile.

Riley stands up, ready to hit the town. "Done?"

When Riley stands up, Julia stops putting on her lipstick. She quickly puts the lipstick back in her purse.

Tracie nods. "Yes."

"Let's go." Julia stands up and leads the way.

Riley and Tracie follow behind. They jog down the stairs towards the back door. They pass through the living room, where Riley's mother and father cuddle on the couch enjoying a romantic movie.

As she approaches the back door, Julia waves to Riley's parents. "Bye."

"Bye Mom, bye Dad," Riley shouts to her parents, just before jolting through the door.

"Don't stay out too late," Riley's Dad says as he watches the girls leave.

"Okay." Riley and Julia rush out.

Straggling quietly behind, Tracie waves at Riley's parents as she leaves. Her smile is simple and quick, and they smile back. Tracie is like a second daughter to them. She and Riley have been best friends since elementary school. Many memories are encased in the walls of this house.

Riley waits in her car as Tracie walks to the driveway. The sounds from the running engine erupt into the air; disturbing the night's silence. Julia sits in the back seat, applying makeup yet again. In her eyes, she can never have too much on. Tracie gets in next to Riley, who does not hesitate to back out of the driveway. The car disappears quickly down the dark street. Unbeknownst to Tracie, this would be her last day as an innocent teenager.

Chapter Two:

The Warning

Riley's car races down the street, with the radio blaring. Riley nods her head to the music as Julia sings along. Julia's pitch is not the most accurate, but at least her lack of vocal ability provides material for a few laughs. Tracie inconspicuously pokes fun at Julia's horrendous rendition of the song under her breath. Tracie prefers to sing along with the song in her head, which in her opinion is what Julia should do.

While Julia sings, her pager begins to beep repeatedly. The paging distracts her from singing, which Tracie thinks is not necessarily a bad thing. She holds her pager up to check the incoming number. Her boyfriend is paging her yet again. One of the many times he has paged her today. Julia scoffs in frustration. At this moment, he is the last person she wants to have a conversation with. Her mood change is undeniable. She has a tumultuous relationship with her boyfriend, and her mood automatically changes each time he contacts her.

Riley looks back at Julia through the rearview mirror. "Who was that?"

Julia does not respond. Riley's question further agitates her.

"Here we go," Tracie mutters to Riley.

"I know." Riley whispers back sarcastically. They both know where this will lead. The combination of immaturity and teenage love are a disaster waiting to happen. Julia's mood swing causes an awkward silence in the car.

Tracie turns back to Julia. "Don't let him ruin our night."

Rendered silent by her frustration with her boyfriend, Julia chooses not to respond. Riley and Tracie are unsure of what to say next.

"Maybe there'll be someone there tonight." Julia peers out the window as she breaks her silence. Julia has the tendency to bounce around between various love interests. This often gets her into more trouble than she can handle. When her boyfriend's actions are less than becoming, she will often find comfort from someone else to temporarily fill the void.

"Yeah, someone cute…for all of us." Riley and Julia laugh. The atmosphere is light again.

"No thanks." Tracie shakes her head. She is not interested in meeting anyone, especially a boy. She has always avoided the opposite sex. This entire conversation is incredibly awkward for her.

"You can't be shy forever. You have to put yourself out there. Live a little." Riley wants Tracie to experiment with the opposite sex, like she and Julia already have. They have never seen Tracie with a boyfriend.

"Just be careful, because you could meet the wrong one like I did." Julia looks out the window at the passing landscape. "It's so obviously wrong, but it feels so incredibly right. I don't know what it is, but you won't be able to break free from a bad boy. You steer clear of the bad ones or you'll be stuck forever. Like me." Julia has had her fair share of bad boys in her short time on this Earth.

"That's what scares me." Tracie says this just low enough to go unheard. Falling for the wrong guy has always scared Tracie. This has always deterred her from dating boys. The fear of the unknown. Even though Tracie is already overly cautious, she reflects deeply on the warning.

Chapter Three:

The Hard Way

Riley pulls into the parking lot of the movie theater. She parks in the closest parking space and turns her car off. The three girls take a moment to do a final check on their hair and makeup before exiting the vehicle. Tracie takes a red lipstick tube out of her purse. She hands it back to Julia, so she can apply additional makeup.

Julia takes the lipstick from Tracie and applies it. "Thanks."

"Are we ready?" Riley is anxious to enter the theater. Tracie nods in agreement.

"You know it." Julia finishes applying her lipstick. She hands the tube back to Tracie.

The three friends get out of the car and walk towards the ticket booth. The ticket booth operator greets them. "How may I help you?" Julia walks up and buys her ticket first.

While waiting for her turn, Tracie becomes uneasy. She is overcome by the feeling of someone looking at her. The sensation lurks in the air all around her. Tracie looks off to her left to confirm her suspicion. She finds a mysterious young male staring at her.

Steve O'Neil, an audacious and suave loner, smokes a cigarette near the entrance of the theater. He slowly blows out smoke, all the while keeping his focus on Tracie. Tracie turns away and blushes. This kind of attention is something she is not accustomed to. Tracie tries to fight the urge to make eye contact, but her curiosity wins the battle. She looks back over in his direction. He has not taken his eyes off of her. He takes another deep puff from his cigarette. After exhaling, he flicks it onto the ground. He turns and walks inside the theater. He looks at Tracie flirtatiously as he disappears inside.

Tracie is smitten by Steve's style and cocky demeanor. He seems daring and bold. This age-old trick continues to work like a charm. He is unlike anyone that has ever given her any attention. Tracie's mother always told her to steer clear from the bad boys on motorcycles who wore leather jackets. Unlike your typical bad boy, Steve has a very polished appearance coupled with his laid back and casual attire. He is not like the guys her mother warned her about. Convincing herself that this unknown admirer is safe, Tracie remains in a daze. Although Steve has already walked into the theater, Tracie cannot take her eyes off the spot where he once stood.

Julia also notices Steve. She is impressed by his physical stature. "Mmm, mmm, mmm."

"What are you mmm, mmm, mmming at?" Riley takes her ticket and joins Tracie and Julia. Tracie feels a little embarrassed about her friends catching her staring at this mysterious guy.

"Ms. Space Cadet is star-struck by her new boyfriend," Julia innocently teases Tracie.

"I am not." Tracie's face turns bright red.

"Some boy toy was standing over there smoking a cigarette and giving her the 'come and get me' face." Julia laughs as she fills Riley in on Tracie's new crush.

"Whatever." Tracie's embarrassment turns to frustration.

"Let's go inside." Riley grabs Tracie by the arm and leads her towards the theater, leaving Julia behind. Riley has decided to drop the conversation so

Tracie will not be uncomfortable. She is sensitive to how painfully shy Tracie is.

"Hey, I thought I was supposed to find a new guy, and the first cute one is all over Tracie…*damn*." Julia runs after Tracie and Riley, who both continue to ignore her. "You're leaving me…really? Are you serious?" Julia finally catches up to them just as they enter the theater. The three girls sit down in one of the middle rows.

"I was only joking." Julia nudges Tracie.

Tracie awkwardly smiles, shrugging Julia off.

"And besides you're a jealous whore…thought you needed to hear that." Riley laughs as she teases Julia.

There is an awkward silence as they wait for Julia's response. The three friends each look at each other, hesitant. Tracie looks from Riley to Julia. Before they know it, all three of them are laughing. Name-calling is a form of endearment among this group of friends.

The lights in the theater slowly dim. The theater is semi-packed. The girls settle down and prepare to watch the previews. As the previews begin, the silhouette of a young male walks up the stairs. The darkness makes it impossible to observe his facial features. He walks right past Tracie and her friends.

This grabs Tracie's attention, because the movie has just started. Everyone should already be in their seats.

The young man sits two rows behind Tracie. Tracie peeks around to see Steve, the young man who stood outside the movie theater staring directly at her. He props his legs on top of the seat in front of him to get her attention. Steve and Tracie immediately catch eyes. He blows her a flirtatious peck. Tracie blushes and quickly turns back around. She grabs her soda and takes a large sip, hoping to regain her composure. While shaking his head, Steve smiles and leans back in his chair. Tracie is eating up his flirtatious gestures, and he knows it. He is slowly reeling her in.

Tracie leans in and whispers to Riley. "He's back there."

Riley turns around and looks. Julia catches wind of what is going on and looks also. They all turn back around and giggle with Tracie. Their giggling agitates the person sitting in front of them, who is trying to watch the movie. Tracie starts to settle down and focus on the movie as well. Uncontrollable laughter fills the theater as the movie, a comedy, plays. Tracie puts her drink into her cup holder. "I'm going to the bathroom," she whispers to her friends.

"Do you want us to come with?" Julia whispers back.

Tracie shakes her head no. She gets up and carefully slides past the other moviegoers.

After washing her hands, Tracie exits the bathroom in a rush. She does not want to miss any more of the movie.

"You sure are walking fast." Steve is standing against the wall by the bathroom door. "And that's okay, but the only problem is you're walking in the wrong direction." Steve looks at Tracie's body intensely. He likes what he sees and he is determined to obtain it at any cost.

"What?" Tracie blushes. She knows what he meant, but decides to play hard to get.

Steve stands up off the wall. He walks over to Tracie. Tracie stands frozen. He has that 'it' factor, inhabiting his body from head to toe.

Steve walks directly up to Tracie, until they are face to face. He strokes Tracie's hair as he pulls her in close. Tracie assumes Steve is going in for their first kiss--at least that is how it appears at first glance. She cannot control her thirst for his lips. She awkwardly prepares for his kiss, not quite sure what to do. Her inexperience is painstakingly clear. Her body and mouth tense up as Steve continues to lean forward. Right before he reaches her lips, he bypasses her face and leans into her ear. He whispers gingerly into Tracie's ear, causing her to tremble.

"Life is funny, ya know. It always has a way of putting you in the right place at the right time." He caresses her face. Tracie blushes, caught up in his charm. Steve gently kisses Tracie's ear. "Just one second too soon or too late, and you might miss that opportunity."

"Opportunity for what?" Tracie is naïve.

Steve strokes Tracie's cheek, then he boldly glides his hand down her chest. His soft touch arouses Tracie instantly. She has never felt this way before. Steve's hand stops right before it reaches her breasts. This is all part of his plan. "Come with me," he whispers in her ear.

Tracie bashfully resists. Steve's advances feel right, but she just cannot act on this temptation without giving it some thought. Snap decisions are out of character for her. She does not like to take risks.

"I can't...my friends." Tracie stutters. She tries to find any excuse to turn Steve down.

Steve is not interested in Tracie's potential excuses. He can see where this is going, and he abruptly interrupts her.

"Look, I understand. You're here with your friends. I respect that." Steve speaks nonchalantly. She is a dime a dozen in his mind. In order to relay this feeling, he turns and walks away. He does not look back at Tracie; not even once. "Hopefully I'll see you again...we'll see what happens." Steve continues to walk away without looking back.

"Wait." Tracie shouts, right before Steve disappears around the corner.

Steve stops in his tracks. Smiling, he keeps his back turned to Tracie. He knows his plan worked. Tracie rushes over to him. "I'm game." Tracie is nervous, but her lust eases any doubts she has about leaving with Steve. "I just have to let my friends know I'm leaving...we all came together. I don't want them to worry." Tracie smiles at Steve as he turns around to face her.

Steve admires Tracie's thoughtfulness. He finds it endearing and attractive. Seeing her rush after him strokes his already colossal ego.

"Go ahead. I'll be waiting out front for you." Steve kisses Tracie quickly and heads for one of the exits. Tracie walks back into the theater and sits next to her friends.

"Where have you been?" Riley has been worried about Tracie. It has been nearly twenty minutes since she left.

"I mean, damn…did you get lost?" Julia leans in, contributing her usual sarcasm.

Tracie laughs this off. "No, I was just talking to a friend."

"A friend? What friend?" Riley does not remember seeing any familiar faces upon entering the theater.

"Umm, I just ran into that really cute guy, and umm, we were just talking."

"Oh my gosh, he's so cute." Julia talks slightly above a whisper. Her tone is unacceptable for a movie theater and it angers the person in front of her. Julia completely disregards the angry man by sticking her tongue out at him.

"I know! And he kissed me," Tracie sighs. The chance at real romance makes her heart flutter. "It was amazing." Tracie smiles from ear to ear.

Julia's heart warms over Tracie's newfound happiness. Tracie is usually shy and withdrawn. Her happiness brings joy to Julia's heart, but Riley does not share this same sentiment. The thought of Tracie interacting with this unknown hoodlum perturbs her. "Well, it doesn't sound that great to me."

"Why would you say that?" Tracie is hurt by Riley's disapproval.

"Cause you don't even know him. I mean what…like really?" Riley's annoyance quickly turns to outrage.

"Why are you getting so angry? I'm just having fun. I'm just doing a little innocent flirting."

Julia tries to help. "Yeah it's just innocent flirting. It's okay to live a little." She can sympathize with Tracie's desire to just have a casual fling. After all, she engages in that kind of behavior herself quite often.

"Look, I'm just going to chill with him." Tracie does not understand why such a big fuss is being made.

"I know, but I just don't want things to get out of control. I just want you to be careful." Riley shows an amount of concern that Tracie has never seen from her before. Tracie finds it alarming. But against the wishes of her close friend, Tracie decides to side with her own desires.

"I will. Bye." Tracie gets up and leaves the theater.

Riley shakes her head in disbelief. She is close to tears. The decision to leave with a stranger is something Tracie would never do. Tracie is behaving completely out of character. Riley sits in her seat, stunned.

"It'll be okay." Julia tries to reassure Riley.

"I would love to believe that Julia. I would, but I have a strong feeling it's not going to be okay." Riley has a tear in her eye.

Tracie can barely contain her excitement. She runs outside, anxiously waiting for Steve. She does not have to wait long. Steve stands in front of his car, which he has parked on the curb directly in front of the theater. He leans against the passenger door confidently, knowing she was going to show up. Tracie beams with joy at the sight of Steve waiting for her. Tracie runs over and leaps into his arms. They greet each other with a passionate kiss. Steve opens the passenger door and helps Tracie in. Tracie could not imagine a better ending; this could really be the fairy tale moment girls dream about. A handsome man waiting to whisk her away to a better life.

As they drive down a busy highway, Steve places his hand on the back of Tracie's head rest. Tracie takes note of Steve's attempts at getting closer to her. Her anxiety increases. They make a right turn onto a street that leads into an obscure, serene park. The park seems deserted, except for a few cars parked at a distance.

The park they are in is a popular and secluded location where young people can spend 'alone time' together. The thick trees provide ample cover for some much-needed privacy. Steve pulls into a parking space and turns the car off. Tracie's nervousness is obvious, but she tries her best to remain composed. She does not want to expose her sexual inexperience.

Steve takes a moment to look deeply into Tracie's eyes. Being a rookie at the art of foreplay, this catches her off guard. She blushes as she tries to look away. Steve leans in and aggressively begins to kiss her. Tracie follows his lead, allowing him to take full control. Right in the middle of their passionate kiss, Steve pulls away. He leans back in the driver's seat. This confuses Tracie, making her believe he has suddenly lost interest. She begins to doubt her decision to leave with him. She looks at him with a confused glare, while Steve continues to look at her in amazement. He undresses her with his eyes, considering every sexual possibility. The passion in his eyes dispels Tracie's suspicion. Steve has not lost interest. He is just savoring every moment. This confirmation of his attraction causes Tracie to blush. She turns her head away, but only for a moment. She turns back around to find Steve still looking directly at her, only now he is smiling. Tracie responds with a flirtatious smile of her own. She looks down at her lap, and timidly bites her lip. Her mind rests amongst the clouds in the sky. She has never felt this way before nor has she received this amount of attention. She eats up every bit of it. Steve's charm has her under a powerful spell. He leans in close and draws Tracie into his arms.

"I feel safe with you...like I can let my guard down," Steve confides. He turns away and looks down. "Do you feel safe with me?" Steve nervously waits.

Tracie answers confidently. "Yes, I feel very comfortable."

"I didn't ask if you were comfortable. Do you feel safe?" Steve asks more firmly.

"Yes," Tracie answers meekly.

Her answer makes Steve feel more confident. He needs Tracie to follow his lead now, so he can take full control later. "You can tell me anything. We can do whatever together. Okay? Only us. I don't want our bond to ever break." Steve's once confident voice collapses with emotion.

"It won't, Steve." Tracie reaches for Steve's hand. She grips its tightly, in an attempt to prove her feelings.

"My attention is on you. That's where it is and that's where it's going to stay." Steve pauses. "Promise me you'll give me the same."

Tracie takes a moment to observe how serious Steve is behaving. She thinks carefully, before she responds. She takes a moment to reflect. Then she nods. "My attention is on you."

That is all Steve needed to hear. He begins to passionately kiss her. It is Tracie's turn to savor every minute of this new encounter. This is exactly where she wants to be: in Steve's arms. Steve pulls Tracie in closer, so she can sit on his lap. She kisses him back, but she allows him to take the lead, which he enjoys very much. Steve roughly snatches off Tracie's shirt and begins to kiss and grope her chest. Steve can no longer control his sexual cravings. He does not want to waste any more time. He decides to move to the next level, whether Tracie is ready or not. He quickly shimmies his pants down to his ankles. Tracie cannot resist the urge to moan.

Steve aggressively inserts himself inside Tracie. Initially, she screams out in pain. The sensation sends shock waves throughout her entire body. She never felt this combination of pleasure and pain before. She begins to pant and breathe heavily. She is nervous and a bit scared, but she welcomes this new and liberating experience.

She slows her breathing and looks down at Steve, who looks up at her with a smile. She giggles out loud, causing Steve to laugh at her. He cannot resist her smile. He moves the hair in her face behind her ears.

"I'm going to take care of you and protect you. You're mine. I promise I will never hurt you." He strokes her hair.

Tracie smiles. "Promise?" She stares into Steve's eyes.

Steve whispers in her ear. "I promise."

Tracie kisses Steve softly on his lips. Steve grabs Tracie's hair and yanks her head back. As Tracie grunts, Steve grabs her neck. He tightens his grip around her throat, constricting her airway. He shows little concern for her choking sounds; in actuality, he enjoys them. They arouse Steve like nothing else ever could. With his arousal at its peak, Steve can act out his secret desires. Steve presses Tracie against the steering wheel. While maintaining his grip on her hair, he begins to thrust himself into her vagina as forcefully as he can. Tracie cries out from the pain.

"I promise…I promise baby." Steve moans under his breath as he thrusts.

Riley tried to advise Tracie to not rush into anything too serious. It would have been best to take her time to get to know Steve, but Tracie made a decision to live her life her way. Despite the warning from her best friend Riley, Tracie decides to learn the hard way.

Chapter Four:

Broken Promises

Tracie stands behind the register in the grocery store where she works. She appears very happy on the surface, but deep in her eyes is a glimpse of sadness. Time and disappointment have aged her face tremendously. It has been fourteen years since the day she first met Steve. If you looked at her face, you would think it had been thirty. A woman pushes her half-full shopping cart to Tracie's checkout line.

"Hi, did you find everything okay?" Tracie scans the woman's items one by one. "Fifty-eight sixty-one is your total."

"Oh shoot, I forgot...duh. I have coupons." The woman reaches into her purse.

Tracie rolls her eyes, but hides her frustration behind a laugh. Later, as her day draws to a close, Tracie breathes a rare sigh of relief. Tracie has been standing for nine hours. The long work hours have taken its toll on Tracie's body. After she checks out her last customer, she turns off her checkout light. She walks away from the register with her purse. She waves at her coworkers on her way to the front door. "Bye, see you tomorrow."

"Stay safe," One of her coworkers calls out.

"I will." She leaves through the sliding doors and scans for her car. After a few moments of searching, she cannot locate the car. Fearing the worst, she assumes her car has been repossessed. She and Steve never have enough money. She has not been able to pay this month's car note. Just as panic begins to set in, Tracie remembers: she had to run errands on her break. She had parked her car in a different parking place. The car is parked safely on the side of the building. She sighs, and chuckles at herself as she walks to her car.

Back at the house, Steve sits on the couch with a cold beer in hand. He, too, has aged dramatically. He is no longer the handsome, charismatic lone wolf he once was. He has gained a substantial amount of weight, due to the safety that resides in complacency.

There are open bags of chips on the couch beside him. Crumbs and empty food wrappers decorate the living room. The living room has become a playroom, with toys scattered all about. The entire place is a mess. Steve focuses his attention on a TV program where women are modeling swimsuits. He takes a large sip of his beer. Distant sounds of a child playing can be heard in the background; as usual, he chooses to ignore them.

Tracie tries to unlock the front door lock, but it is jammed. The lock is weathered and often jams. Tracie always has a hard time getting in. Most of the house is on its last leg, due to a lack of resources and Steve's refusal to do any maintenance activities. The lock finally loosens, after almost a minute of struggling. Tracie enters the house. This house is no longer a home. Observing her surroundings, she finds a complete disaster. Toys, food, and clothes are everywhere. The kitchen sink and counter are littered with dishes. Every area of the house is in complete disarray. The house did not look this way when she left. She turns to Steve, who is still unaware of her arrival.

"Hello." Tracie crosses her arms and scowls.

Steve slowly turns his head towards Tracie, projecting the illusion of acknowledgement. He does not want to take his eyes off the swimsuit models. "What's for dinner?" He immediately turns back around to face the TV.

Tracie's rage boils to the surface. Steve's consistent lack of support leaves her feeling belittled and taken for granted. She takes an aggressive tone without considering the potential consequences. "Well, maybe you could have fixed dinner or picked something up. I've been at work all day. I mean, really."

"What?" Steve rises to his feet, beer in hand. He walks around the couch towards her. Tracie falls into a regretful silence.

"What did you say?" Steve asks more loudly this time, and with a more threatening inflection. He stands directly in front of Tracie.

"I---I was just saying the house is mess." Tracie realizes she should have gauged his mood before confronting him.

"Oh it is? Well I guess you want it cleaned right?" Steve chugs the rest of his beer. He crushes the can with one hand and flings it on the ground. Then in one swift motion, he knocks Tracie to the ground. "Then why don't you clean it? All that time you spent talking, it could have been cleaned by now." Steve is shouting now.

While holding her face, Tracie looks up at Steve. She sucks her mouth in tightly to stifle the cries. Steve stands over Tracie, taking offense at her looking at him. If she has the nerve to lay eyes on him after the way she addressed him, he does not think she has learned her lesson. "You got something else to say?"

Cowering, Tracie shakes her head no. She turns her face toward the floor, crying silently so that Steve cannot hear. Crying sometimes angers Steve, making the beatings last longer.

"That's what I thought." Steve walks out of the room.

Once Steve is a safe distance away, Tracie cannot hold back her sobs. She remains on the floor, with tears rolling down her face.

When Tracie met her husband, he said he would protect and love her. He promised that he would never cause her any harm, and she believed him. Even in her wildest nightmare, she could not imagine that their entire existence would be made up of broken promises.

Chapter Five:

A Mother's Sacrifice

The next day at work, Tracie wears an unusual amount of makeup. She usually opts for a 'natural' look, since her limited income makes makeup a luxury. Lucky for her, she has the next two days off. She hopes to make it through the day without anyone noticing the bruise on her left cheek. She is in the breakroom hoping to stay under the radar when Sandra, a friend and coworker, walks in. Sandra immediately notices the difference in Tracie's makeup.

"What's his name?"

"Whose name?" Tracie keeps her face hidden.

"The man you're cheating with? I'm just saying you've got to be cheating, if you're walking around here looking that good."

Initially taken aback, Tracie quickly realizes that Sandra was only teasing. She lets down her guard. "No, I just wanted to try a new look." Laughing at the joke, she unwittingly turns around and exposes her left cheek.

"Well I like it. The only thing is on this cheek, you used too much blush." She playfully brushes Tracie's left cheek, too quickly for Tracie to react. Then she gasps. "Your face---what happened?" Sandra's mind races with explanations for why Tracie's face would be bruised. Her genuine concern makes Tracie tense up defensively. Tracie's reaction instantly brings Sandra to the most apparent conclusion.

"I don't wanna talk about it." Tracie brushes past her and walks out of the break room.

"Tracie…Tracie." Sandra chases after her.

Tracie storms away, which only increases her coworker's suspicion. Sandra has a feeling that something is not right. She does not want to offend Tracie, but she decides that she cannot let the situation go. She could never live with herself if she did not stand up for a friend who could not stand up for herself. She pulls out her cellphone.

Tracie walks to her register and begins her shift. Sandra walks past Tracie's checkout line hoping to get her attention, but Tracie refuses to make any eye contact with her.

Back at home, Steve is passed out on the couch with the TV at nearly maximum volume. There are beer cans on the coffee table, and on the floor near the couch. There is a knock at the door that would wake any sober person, but between the blaring television and his alcoholic binge, Steve continues to sleep. Eventually, the banging rouses him and he stumbles to his feet. His head is pounding from a developing hangover.

Steve slowly cracks open the door to poke his head out. He finds a police officer standing on his doorstep. Unimpressed, Steve stares at the officer blankly.

"I need to have a word with you for a moment. Can I come in?"

Steve pauses for a moment, then responds defiantly. "For what?"

"I wanna ask you about your wife's face." The officer smirks.

"No, you definitely can't come in."

"I expected that." The officer's posture tenses as his tone becomes more threatening. "I got my suspicions about what's really going on in this house." He leans in closer. "And I'm going to be watching you like a hawk."

Steve laughs off the policeman's scare tactics. "You're watching me...interesting." Steve pauses. "I'll make sure to put on a show, then." Steve slams the door as hard as he can.

Back at the store, Tracie completes another stressful work shift. She grabs her purse and rushes out of the grocery store. Tracie is once again relieved to see that her car is still in the parking lot. She hears Sandra's voice behind her. "Tracie---Tracie." Sandra catches her just as she is about to get into her car. Tracie turns around.

"Hey I wanted to catch you before you left so I could check on you. You alright?" Sandra is breathing heavily from chasing after her.

"Yeah, Yeah, I'm good." Tracie is anxious to get away.

"Well, I'm here for you if you ever want to leave. I'll help you." Sandra pauses. "I called my brother...he went to your house." She braces for Tracie's response.

"What! I love him. Why did you do that?!" Tracie begins to panic.

"We wanted to make sure you were okay." Sandra knows Tracie would have never called the police on her own.

"I can't believe you did that." Tracie is furious. She gets in her car. She slams the door shut and starts the engine.

While shouting out her name, Sandra frantically bangs on Tracie's car window. She desperately tries to get her attention. Tracie shifts into drive and floors it. She peels out of the parking lot without giving Sandra a chance to finish explaining.

Tracie fiddles with her keychain as she rushes to her front door. Tracie is a very private and secretive person. This embarrassing part of her private life being exposed hurts her deeply. She walks into the house and puts her purse down on the kitchen table. Shortly after, she hears a faint scream.

As Tracie walks down the hallway, the screams grow louder. She does not feel overly-surprised; she has become numb to Steve's violence. As she reaches the door of her son's room, she hears a loud smack followed by a thud on the floor. She bursts through the door to find her young son Austin on the floor, bleeding from the nose.

Usually meek, Tracie is overcome with rage. Until this point Steve has only hit Tracie--at least to her knowledge. Austin sobs uncontrollably on the ground. He clinches his nose to try and stop the blood. Tracie has a rush of strength and courage. She can tolerate the physical abuse, but she will not stand around to see her children suffer the same fate. This is where she draws the line. She grabs Austin's baseball bat from near the door. Without thinking twice, she swings the bat at Steve. The bat hits him in the upper back.

Tracie is caught off guard when Steve stumbles but remains standing. She was hoping the hit would knock him out.

Steve turns around and charges at Tracie. She drops the bat and flees the room. Steve catches up with her and tackles her in the hallway. He stands over her, straddling her as she tries to stand. She manages to make it to all fours, but Steve kicks her directly in the stomach. The kick steals all the fight from Tracie. She begins to sob loudly. She uses the small amount of strength she has left to curl into a fetal position, anticipating more kicks to her body. The fetal position has been her primary defense for years now.

"You really think a cop is going to scare me?" Steve balls up his fists. "Why in the hell did a cop come to my fuckin' front door?" He kicks her again, this time with more force. "You bring cops to my door and think you're going to scare me?" He kicks her in the side. Tracie begins to cough uncontrollably.

Blood begins to expel from her mouth, but Steve is not done with her. He grabs her by the hair and drags her down the hallway, back towards the living room.

Austin stands outside his bedroom door, watching his father drag his mother by the hair. He is emotionless as he watches this violent attack. He is also accustomed to this level of violence in the household. Then he hears his mother scream.

Austin has never heard his mother scream. As he thinks about it, he has never heard his mother make any noise during Steve's beatings. She has always taken the beatings in silence, never wanting her children to know she was afraid or in pain. Austin begins to scream for his mother. She does not respond. Steve drags Tracie to the living room and yanks her up to her feet.

Tracie looks over at her son, who is watching with tears in his eyes. "Go back in the room," she directs him.

Austin follows his mother's instructions and goes back into his room. Tracie's continuous struggling causes Steve to lose his grip of her.

Her will to fight enrages Steve. A message must be sent. He smacks her across the face. She stumbles into the dining room table.

In his bedroom, Austin slides down the door and rests his back against it. The sounds of his mother being thrown against the wall ricochet throughout the entire house. Her hopeless screams break Austin's heart. He covers his ears with his hands, as his tears flow for the mother he loves.

The next morning, Austin is still asleep on the floor. He had sat by his bedroom door, waiting for an end to the violent episode between his parents, until his eyes could no longer stay open. The bruises on his right cheek have now turned purple. The right side of his face is slightly swollen. The rips in his shirt reflect the struggle from the night before. Along with his new scars, he has old ones on his body, legs, and shoulders. They are all battle wounds from previous encounters with his dad. These bruises are also secrets he has kept from his mother. He has kept these secrets for fear of his father's retaliation.

Though Austin is twelve years old, he could easily pass for eight. His legs and arms are lanky, and his face is sunken in from a lack of nourishment. His bones are conspicuous to the eye. Money is always tight, which means food can be scarce. A bed and a few toys are his only possessions in his irreparable world. Poverty is his way of life--the only way of life he knows.

Steve sits on the couch: his favorite spot in the house. He spills some liquor onto the coffee table as he pours a glass. He drinks what is in the glass in one sip. He wastes no time pouring another glass. The glass is empty in seconds. The speed with which he drinks causes him to miss his mouth. Alcohol runs down his face and neck. The strong liquor burns as it runs down his throat. He coughs from the stinging sensation. Steve continues to chug, though the sun has only been in the sky for a few hours.

Tracie walks into their only bathroom, located in the hallway. She looks into the mirror and examines her battered face. The sight of the bruises and cuts breaks her already fragile heart. Tears run from her right eye; they cannot run from her left eye, because it is swollen shut. Her tears sting the open wounds on her face, making her cringe. Her modest frame has taken all the abuse it can handle. The beating she endured the night before would have been fatal to most women her size, but Tracie has gotten tough over the years. Her heart has hardened as well, due to the damage Steve has continued to do to her body.

Tracie opens the medicine cabinet and grabs the rubbing alcohol. It seems like every day; she is cleansing a new cut. The beatings are becoming more frequent. A bandage is wrapped around her left wrist.

She gently swabs her face with a washcloth, in an attempt to cleanse her latest bloody cuts. She squirms as the alcohol touches each wound. She bravely fights through the pain, because she has to get her face back to normal before she can return to work. She cannot afford for anyone else to question her unstable home life. The next time might be her last.

"Tracie. Where you at, girl?" Steve shouts from the living room.

Steve's shouts startle Tracie. She drops the bottle of rubbing alcohol and bloody washcloth in a panic. The rubbing alcohol splashes on the sink and the floor, as Tracie rushes out to Austin's bedroom. Frantic, she finds Austin still asleep on the floor. She yanks him up out of his sleep. She wants him to hide.

"Get in the closet, baby. Mommy needs you stay in here." Tracie kisses Austin and forces him in the closet.

"Mommy what's going on? I'm scared."

Tracie strokes Austin's hair in an attempt to reassure him. Even though the environment is tense and potentially explosive, Tracie is still a mother first. It is difficult, but she tries to shield them from as much of the violence as she can. "No---No baby, everything is going to be fine. Just stay here and don't move." Tracie looks in the closet and then back at Austin. "You guys have to stay here. Okay?"

Austin nods his head and begins to cry. Steve's shouts grow louder.

"I love you so much. Don't either of you move." Tracie closes the closet door and rises to her feet. She makes her way to the bedroom door. She does not want Steve to attack her in front of the children. She would rather the violence happen in the living room, away and out of their sight.

"Tracie. Where the fuck are you?" Steve shouts at the top of his lungs.

Tracie knows what is coming next. Steve is not finished. Another confrontation is inevitable, so she decides to confront him first. She wanted it to happen away from the children, but it is too late.

Steve opens the door with a single, powerful kick. The top hinge flies off, but the bottom hinge still clings loosely to the mount of the door. Tracie is startled by this and jumps back. Another step closer and the door would have hit her. Her back faces the closet. She is the only thing standing between her children and imminent danger.

"Didn't you hear me calling you, bitch? I knew you were dumb, but I guess we can add deaf to the list also." Steve sips from a bottle of alcohol as he walks towards her.

Tracie backs away in disgust. She makes sure not to back up near the closet. With nowhere else to go, she bumps into a wall. Steve takes a long, hearty sip from his bottle and places it on an end table near Austin's bed. Tracie cannot read Steve's personality; he appears blank to her, neither angry nor happy. Tracie takes a gamble.

"I was just trying to clean up," Tracie stammers. She hopes this will please him. Steve loves to see Tracie clean. He calmly looks at Tracie. His moods can switch on and off like a light. Tracie breathes a deep sigh of relief, but the relief only lasts momentarily. In a flash, his hands are around her throat and she is pinned against the wall.

"You know; I could crush you with my bare hands. I own you, the kids, everything." Steve tightens his grip around her neck.

Tracie tries to squirm away. Austin peers out of the closet. He watches his father choke his mother. He sits in the closet, filled with terror and hopelessness. He cannot help his mother. His parents' constant battling brings depression and sadness to his heart.

"You're hurting me. Let me go."

"I'm not hurting you yet," Steve yells directly into Tracie's face. Tracie's continued wriggling enrages him even more. Resisting his attacks is completely out of the ordinary for her. He slaps her face with every ounce of his strength, knocking her to the floor. The slap reopened some of the cuts on her face. Before Tracie can get back up, Steve sits on her chest. Then, he proceeds to deliver punch after punch to her body. She tries to swing back, but her efforts are useless.

In shock, Austin watches from the closet. He turns away, wanting it to disappear as if it were a dream he could wake up from. He looks back to confirm that this is not a dream. This is his reality. He looks out the closet and scans the room. He sees a bottle of alcohol sitting on the end table. "He's going to kill us if we don't do something," he whispers to himself. He can no longer stand back and watch this happen in front of him. Even at his young age, he understands that his decision is dangerous and could make things much worse...so it is all or nothing. He decides he has to go for it.

Austin slowly reaches for the door handle, and pushes it open as quietly as he can. His only chance is to catch his father off guard. He crawls out of the closet, focused despite his pounding heart. He slowly makes his way to the liquor bottle sitting on the end table, when doubt begins to creep into his mind.

Steve begins to choke Tracie more severely. She gags loudly, gasping and struggling for every breath. Austin watches his mother kick and struggle. Then, he looks back at the bottle of liquor. His mind jumps back and forth. And then suddenly, he remembers an incident with his father. It replays in his mind, as clearly as if it had happened yesterday.

About a month ago, Austin was playing innocently in his room. He felt a swift backhand across his face. He immediately fell motionless to the ground. About an hour later, Steve walked over to Austin's unconscious body and dumped a bucket of water on his head. Austin jumped up, confused and startled. "Get up. You're not gonna sleep on my floor all day." Steve dropped the bucket next to Austin and walked away.

While remembering this unprovoked attack, a sense of power rushes through Austin. The memory enrages him. He stands up straight. With newfound assertion, he grabs the liquor bottle from the end table. He rushes at his father with hate in his heart. He shatters the bottle over Steve's head. He cautiously steps back awaiting the reaction from his belligerent father.

Steve gets up off Tracie. He stumbles around in pain and shock, looking for the person who hit him. He turns around to see Austin. He touches his head, then examines the blood on his hand in disbelief. He stares at Austin.

"Leave my mother alone. Enough is enough." Austin stands firmly.

"You just signed your death certificate, boy." Steve charges at Austin.

Tracie reaches out and grabs Steve's ankle, catching just enough to make him tumble to the floor.

"Run. Get Out." Tracie motions for her son to leave.

Austin runs to the bedroom door. He looks back at his mother with tears in his eyes. Steve gets up and refocuses his rage on Tracie.

"Go!" She motions more aggressively for Austin to leave. Steve grabs her by the hair, jerking her head back. Tracie screams in agony as Austin runs out of the room.

Within minutes, police cars swarm the neighborhood. Calls had been placed by various neighbors who heard the screams. Police officers rush to Austin's aid and try their best to calm him down. He is far too hysterical, so they lead him to awaiting paramedics. The police officer that visited Steve a couple of days ago leads a team of officers into the house.

Neighbors rush out of their homes to see what the commotion is about. The middle-aged couple across the street are outside their home, holding each other.

Inside, the lead officer finds Steve standing in the hallway. He wants to make sure he is the one who places this monster under arrest. Surprisingly, Steve does not fight or resist in any capacity. Instead, he smiles as he waits to be handcuffed. "You're under arrest." He yanks Steve by the arm.

Steve laughs out loud. "You didn't believe me, did you?" Steve tries to make eye contact, but the officer keeps his focus on applying the cuffs.

"Let's go." He shoves Steve toward the door.

Steve turns around. His expression radiates evil. He looks the officer directly in the eyes. "I told you I was going to put on a show." Steve is covered in Tracie's blood. The neighbors gasp as a team of officers escorts him out the door and to a squad car. The mood in the neighborhood goes from panic to heartbreak as they watch intently.

Austin now is calm in the back of the ambulance. Reality has sunken in. He sifts through the stares in the crowd, and manages to catch the eye of a little girl across the street. She looks at him through a downstairs window. Their shared gaze is long and somber, but comforting for Austin. It is a stare she will remember for the rest of her life.

A team of investigators roll two body bags, one large and one small, to a coroner's van at the curb. Austin does not notice the bags. His attention is on the man who took his mother from him. That man was not his father. He never was and never will be. He vows to never utter his name again. As Steve is driven away in the police car, Austin follows with a cold stare. Despite his loss, he feels freedom and relief deep inside. A weight has been lifted from his shoulders. He had escaped a near-fatal episode, all because of a mother's sacrifice.

Chapter Six:

Behind the Mask

Austin sits across from his psychologist, Dr. Gary Morgan, during his weekly visit. Dr. Morgan is a successful, well known therapist. His office exudes prestige. Following the death of his mother Austin started receiving treatment from Dr. Harry Morgan. Throughout the years Austin has been prescribed a slew of medications to help temper his violent mood swings. These mood swings are a result of witnessing the savage acts deriving out of his childhood. Austin continues his recommended therapy appointments with great reluctance.

Austin has a polished appearance: his chocolate brown hair is styled perfectly, and his clothes are in immaculate condition. The most intriguing thing about him is his chiseled, meticulous bone structure.

Over the past eight years, he has become an exact replica of his father. Yet despite his impressive appearance, Austin is numb and morose. He has no concept of true happiness.

"I see it over and over again. I can't get it out of my head." Austin rubs his forehead and eyes as he feels himself tensing up.

"What exactly is it that you can't get out of your head?" Dr. Morgan jots down some notes. Austin has been his patient for three months, and their relationship has grown steadily.

Austin hangs his head low. Looking in mirrors has always been an issue for him. Every line and feature in his face reminds him of the man who once was his father, and this frightens him. Austin has not spoken to or seen Steve since that tragic day. He refuses to. The image of his father's smiling face, moments after he killed his mother, haunts him daily.

"His face terrorizes me in my sleep."

"Terrorizes? What do you see in your sleep?"

"At first all I saw was just flashes, but recently…" Austin sighs. "It's everything. I see everything happen all over again, as if I'm there. I always wake up seeing that *fucking grin* on his face." Austin can no longer hold back his emotions.

Dr. Morgan allows Austin some time to regain his composure. "And once you wake up, how do you feel?" Dr. Morgan remains calm, and sets down his pen and paper. "Whatever you want to say, or want to share, completely depends on you. So you can take as much time as you need to compose yourself." He leans in closer. "It's okay to say whatever you feel like sharing. No one will judge you." Dr. Morgan leans back.

"When I see my mother being attacked, I feel so helpless." Austin balls his fists in anger. The same way his father used to. "I want to do something, but I can't...I want to do something, but I can't. Then I get so angry sometimes, I can hardly control myself." His chest heaves in and out.

Dr. Morgan senses the coming breakthrough, and wisely chooses not to interrupt. Austin sits forward in his chair. He has not made eye contact with Dr. Morgan yet in this conversation.

"I'm watching my father attack my mother and I'm terrified, ya know. I'm in the closet watching this happen, and I can't do anything to help my mom." Austin pauses. Dr. Morgan takes the opportunity to jot down some quick notes.

"As I'm watching, I get the urge to do something." Austin's voice becomes more firm.

Dr. Morgan looks up from his notes and pulls down his glasses. "Uh Huh."

"I get this uncontrollable urge to help my mother. And before I know it I hit him." Austin blurts out his confession.

"You hit your father?"

Austin nods. Dr. Morgan looks down and thumbs through Austin's file. He looks up at Austin, confused by the discrepancies. But the questions will have to wait; their session has come to an end.

Austin leaves Dr. Morgan's office. He walks out of the building. He steps aside by the front door to have a smoke and calm down. He breathes deeply in and out as he smokes. The feeling of stress slowly begins to evaporate. Austin takes one last puff of his cigarette. Just as he flicks the butt on the ground, he notices a very attractive woman walking in his direction. She is walking towards the office building. Beautiful is an understatement. She struts past Austin with a confidence that demands his attention. She smirks as he turns his head and watches her walk by.

"You see something you like?" She winks and bats her eyes. She smiles at Austin as she enters the building.

Austin chuckles, but is not interested in pursuing the invitation. He walks out to the front row of the parking lot and finds his car. As he pulls his car keys from his pocket, a prescription pill bottle falls to the ground. In it are the pills which control Austin's daily, violent mood swings. He chuckles as he picks up the pill bottle. He reads the label one last time before he arrogantly tosses it back on the ground. He gets in his car and begins the hour long commute to the mail delivery company where he works. When he arrives, he slings a gym bag over his shoulder and heads for the back door of the building. All employees must enter through the employee door in back, using individual employee codes.

Once inside, he goes to the bathroom to put on his uniform. He grabs his assigned clipboard off the wall and walks over to his work station. Beneath his work station is the locker where he routinely stores his gym bag. Austin puts the bag safely inside. He skims through the clipboard to check his delivery route for the day. He reaches for his work belt and detaches an electronic scanner, which he uses to scan a stack of boxes.

Austin's coworker Jason enters the room and walks over to Austin. "Hey man, what's going on?" Jason greets him with a friendly swat on the back.

Austin turns around and smiles. Jason's awkward, good-humored nature can always lighten a room.

"So what happened this weekend?" Jason's wild weekends usually provide entertainment on slow Monday mornings. Jason's grin lets Austin know his weekend was entertaining.

"Man let me tell you: wow." Jason whistles. "I mean; I was with the hottest girl. I mean titties, ass...mmm, perfect."

"You lying son of a bitch."

"No, seriously, this babe was oozing sex appeal." Jason caresses his own chest, mimicking a large bosom.

"My point exactly. Any woman with that much sex appeal isn't doing anything with you." They both laugh.

"Okay, maybe she just walked past me." Jason turns and walks back to his work station.

"Yeah, that's what I thought." Austin laughs as he continues scanning boxes.

The warehouse manager walks into the back storage room. Outraged by the sound of laughter, he shouts at Jason and Austin to start their delivery routes. He is a stout, homely man who makes up for his stature with overbearing negativity. He is frequently profane, and he is not fond of Jason and Austin's overall work performance. He rolls his eyes and exits the room.

Jason waves his middle finger tauntingly at the door. "Asshole." Austin breaks into a fit of laughter.

"Okay, I'm out of here." Austin heads for the dolly machine, where the packages he must deliver for the day are stacked to be loaded on the truck. He pushes a shipment through the rear door. He walks the shipment towards his delivery truck in the parking lot. To the average eye, Austin appears to be nothing short of ordinary. Most people would see Austin as a law-abiding citizen, but something else lurks behind the mask.

Chapter Seven:

Her Life Will Never Be the Same

A vibrant young woman named Kasey drives into the garage of Campbell & Associates, one of the most influential law firms in Seattle. Kasey keeps her body in superior condition. Her hair and nails are always in compliance with her wardrobe. She traditionally favors pink lipstick and nail polish but experiments frequently with her makeup. To Kasey, image is everything.

She gives herself a quick touchup in the rearview mirror. As she applies mascara, her hand slips and creates a small black streak across her nose. This infuriates her. Anything that might negatively alter her appearance is potentially devastating. Her confidence and mood are dependent on how she is perceived. She removes the mascara from her nose. She picks up her coffee and takes a sip while still looking in the mirror. Multitasking leads her to inadvertently spill coffee on her tailored suit and shirt. She takes a deep breath as her frustration soars.

"Okay, I'm not going to break. Everything's fine. I'm going to walk into work and everything will be alright."

Kasey takes a deep breath before getting out of her car. She walks towards the door which opens to a stairwell. This stairwell leads to a side entrance of the law firm. She usually chooses this entrance, because it is the quickest route to her desk. Kasey is almost finished with her undergraduate degree. Her dream of being a successful prosecutor has led her to work with this prominent law firm.

Inside the firm, Jennifer stands at the receptionist's desk. She sifts through a short stack of papers. Highly educated and health conscious, Jennifer exudes confidence and professionalism. This, along with her focus and ambition, is how she has become a partner at the firm despite only being twenty-nine.

Kasey enters the office and walks towards her work area, where Jennifer stands. Jennifer immediately senses Kasey's increasing frustration.

Jennifer smiles at Kasey. "Good morning."

Kasey mutters hello.

"Is everything okay?" Jennifer thinks she already knows the answer.

"Umm yeah. Why do you ask?" Kasey walks past Jennifer.

"Umm, maybe because I'm your best friend and I know when you're bullshitting." She follows Kasey to her desk.

"It's just one of those days. You know, just when everything goes wrong. Like one thing after another." Kasey puts her purse and tote bag on the ground, then flops onto her chair. Her body gradually sinks into the chair.

Jennifer sympathizes with Kasey's frustration. She began as Kasey's mentor a year ago, but the two became fast friends. They have been close ever since.

"I know those days always come, but they always go. Remember that. You know something great always happens if you can make it through the bad days." Jennifer bends down and hugs Kasey.

Kasey smiles, feeling calmed. Encouragement and love were scarce in Kasey's childhood. Kasey grew up in a cold orphanage that did not provide adequate guidance and affection. She chooses to suppress the vague memories of physical and sexual abuse caused by her parents. Kasey has always yearned for love and support from a mother figure, and Jennifer fills this long-standing void.

"You always know what to say. Thank you. I don't know what I would do without you."

"I know. I'm just going to start billing you for all my services." Jennifer chuckles. Kasey's laugh follows closely behind.

"Anyway, here you go." Jennifer hands Kasey a list of her daily duties.

"Ah...my favorite part of the day. My master's orders." Kasey laughs dispassionately as she takes the agenda.

"Well, you know it's Mr. Campbell's way or the highway. And those right over there." Jennifer points to a pile of papers on Kasey's desk. "Those all need to be filed before the eleven o'clock meeting." Jennifer uses hand motions to stress the importance of the work Kasey needs to get done. Kasey makes a whipping sound, and an accompanying whipping motion with her hand.

"Okay. I'll get right on it." Kasey turns to face her computer.

Jennifer begins to walk down the hallway back to her office. At the same moment, Austin walks towards the reception desk with a package in his hand. Focused on her assignments, Kasey is completely unaware of Austin's approach.

As he approaches the reception desk, he looks up to see Kasey. Her beauty immediately catches his attention. He is even a bit rattled, as he pauses to admire Kasey from afar. Despite his troubled past, Austin exudes an audacious confidence that masks his many flaws. Wherever he goes, he always manages to leave a lasting impression. He continues to stare at Kasey, like a lion staring at its prey. He waits for the right moment to pounce.

Kasey is interrupted by the uneasy sense of being stared at. She looks up to find a delivery man standing at her desk.

"Can I help you?" Kasey asks with a raised eyebrow. She is annoyed, but she remains professional.

"You most certainly can." Austin continues to stare. Kasey senses his attraction.

"Okay, so tell me what I can help you with so I can do it and send you on your way."

Despite her lack of interest, Austin is unmoved. He is determined to dodge any possible rejection. Just like his father did, on the night when he reeled in his mother at the movie theater. Austin continues to flirt.

"I have a package here for Mr. Campbell. I need his signature." Austin places the package on Kasey's desk. He pulls out his electronic signature pad.

"Okay, well you can leave the package here, and I'll sign for it." Kasey reaches for the signature pad. Austin places it in her hand. Kasey signs the pad quickly, so Austin can be on his way.

"Feel free to write down your number as well." Austin leans on Kasey's desk.

Kasey's eyebrow raises. "Really?" She stands up. Her body language becomes more welcoming. Austin's excitement is at an all-time high as Kasey leans in closer. The tension rises as she whispers in his ear.

"Feel free to leave at any time." Kasey grins slyly.

Austin feels slightly embarrassed as Kasey smirks and sits back down. He laughs disdainfully.

"Okay…okay, shutdown. That's okay. I get it. Well, I'll leave my number. I'm Austin, by the way." Austin takes a business card from his pocket. He places it on Kasey's desk, right in front of her.

Kasey glances at the card without interest. She turns her attention back to her computer. Austin spots a small vase of carnations on Kasey's desk. The carnations are dry and wilted from a lack of attention. He also notices a pile of business cards for the law firm. He slips one into his pocket without Kasey noticing.

"It wouldn't hurt to use that card some time." Austin smiles at Kasey.

Kasey keeps her attention on her keyboard. "Goodbye."

Austin turns and walks away. He looks back in hopes of exchanging a final glance, but to no avail. Austin exits out of the building. He walks back to his delivery truck to continue his route. Kasey does not know it at the time, but as of this moment her life will never be the same.

Chapter Eight:

Plant A Seed

Kasey shuts down her computer, thankful for the end of her work day. She turns off the light on her desk. She grabs her purse, cell phone, and tote bag. She scans her desk one last time to make sure she has not left anything. Just as she is about to leave, the phone rings. Still technically on the clock for a few minutes, she answers reluctantly.

"Campbell and Associates. How may I help you?"

"You didn't call."

"Excuse me?" Kasey does not recognize the voice.

"I gave you my card today...Austin. I was hoping to hear your beautiful voice again."

Kasey remembers him, and her patience vanishes immediately. She scoffs, rolling her eyes in disgust. "Look, I told you I'm not interested."

Austin senses her frustration, and another possible rejection. He turns on the sweet talk.

"Is that anyway to talk to a secret admirer? You know what I just thought of? You haven't told me your name. You know how rude it is to have a conversation without giving your name? And you are definitely too beautiful to be so rude. Can I put a name to that beautiful face?" Austin's calm, seductive tone keeps Kasey on the phone. All she wants to do is end the conversation, but her mood is slowly shifting.

"It's Kasey."

"Kasey---hmmm. Kasey. That's so pretty. It matches you perfectly." Kasey stumbles out a thank you and falls silent.

"Now that I know your first name, maybe we could have a nice quiet dinner. Hopefully at that dinner I can make you comfortable enough that you can give me your last name." Austin's suave charisma is an inherited trait from his ghastly father.

"You just don't quit, do you?" Kasey giggles. Her concern and worry melt away. She starts to soften.

"I didn't hear an answer."

"I'll think about it. That's the best I can do. Now if you'll excuse me, I have to go."

Austin interjects quickly. "Kasey, don't forget to think about our date. I'll see you soon."

"Goodbye." Kasey hangs up the phone.

In an odd and unexpected way, Kasey's day is brightened. She walks away from the reception desk with an extra spring in her step. Austin has left a lasting, subconscious impression on Kasey. This is a skill he has mastered over the years. As a master of his craft, he waters his dreams. He patiently waits for it to grow, but the garden of love can only begin after you plant a seed.

Chapter Nine:

A Blossom of Love

While sitting on the edge of his bed, Austin places his phone back on its cradle on his night stand. He just got done charming Kasey over the phone. He lies back, with his hands crossed behind his head. His confidence is at an all-time high, and he is sure he will see Kasey again. In order to guarantee this outcome, he knows he needs to be more aggressive.

Austin turns to glance at an old family photo on the nightstand. The family in this photo glimmers with happiness. They appear to be the perfect, happy American family, but to Austin, this photo represents a lot of pain. Even though the photo represents pain, he keeps it as motivation to perform a personal quest. He stands and makes his way to the bathroom. On his way, he passes a wall that is covered with newspaper articles. The articles include an announcement of his father's arrest, an announcement of his father's death sentence, and a eulogy from his mother's funeral. Over time, this wall has become a shrine. This shrine is a reminder of the day that changed him forever. Austin lacks the wherewithal to understand that a constant reminder of that tragic day is only damaging him mentally and emotionally. With every passing day, his condition worsens.

As he walks into the bathroom, Austin feels dizzy. His body has started to go through the beginning stages of withdrawal. Austin has not taken any form of medication in days. He drinks a cupful of tap water. Then, he takes his routine shower before going to bed for the night.

The next morning at work, Kasey makes coffee in the break room. She had an unusually restless night. Needing a 'pick me up', she chugs the coffee quickly despite its nearly scalding temperature. She walks over to the copy machine and starts to copy a large stack of papers.

Felecia, a new intern at the firm, enters the room where Kasey is making copies. She looks around nervously. It is her first day on the job, and she was told that Kasey Laine is going to show her the ropes. Her mission right now is to find Kasey Laine.

When Kasey hears someone enter the room, she turns around to see Felecia. She utters a casual greeting before turning around to resume copying. Felecia walks over to her and extends her hand. "Hi, I'm Felecia."

Kasey accepts her handshake. "I'm Kasey."

"Oh, great. Jennifer told me you were going to train me today. It's my first day."

"Oh. Well, okay. I'm just copying some files for Mr. Campbell. We can get started after I finish. You can have some coffee or a pastry while you wait for me." Kasey points to the refreshment area.

"Oh thanks." Felecia grabs a cup of coffee and drinks it awkwardly. Her nerves are rattled. She wants to make a good first impression on her first day.

Kasey turns around and continues working. "So where are you from?"

"I was born in Mount Vernon, but I moved here to Seattle a little while back. I'm studying law at Seattle University."

"That's impressive; law school." Kasey finishes her copying. "We can head to my desk now." With Felecia close behind, Kasey leads the way from the break room to the reception area.

"I'm in my first semester right now. It's a lot of work, but I like it. Where are you from?"

"Well, I'm a Seattle native. A pretty monotonous life," Kasey laughs. She places the stack of papers onto her desk. Then, she pulls up another chair so they both can sit. Kasey turns on her computer and logs in. "The system is fairly simple. Now, learning where everything is, that's the trick." She smiles, trying to reassure her nervous trainee. Feeling relieved, Felecia chuckles.

Kasey gestures toward her computer. "This right here is our mainframe. We use this for everything. Meetings, budgets..." Kasey is interrupted by a delivery man's arrival at her desk. He is holding carnations.

"I have a delivery for a Ms. Kasey."

"That's me, I'm Kasey." Kasey does not generally receive deliveries at work.

"Here you go ma'am." The delivery man hands Kasey the carnations and card. Then, he extends a clipboard. "Just sign on the last line ma'am." Kasey signs reluctantly.

"Have a nice day."

"You do the same." Admiring the carnations, Kasey blushes like a young girl receiving her first Valentine.

"Are those from your boyfriend?" Felecia smirks.

"I don't have a boyfriend." Kasey is embarrassed.

"Well, someone has a secret admirer."

Jennifer notices the delivery man from down the hall. She walks over to Kasey's desk.

"Whose flowers are those?"

"They're mine," Kasey teases and boasts simultaneously.

Jennifer laughs crudely. "You don't have a man, so someone must be hoeing around and I don't know about it." Kasey gasps.

Felecia tries to laugh away her discomfort. "She has a secret admirer."

"Oh, really." Jennifer enjoys this type of banter, but Kasey has had enough. With a point of her finger, she warns Jennifer to stop.

"Okay, Okay. All fun and games." Jennifer directs her attention to Felecia. "I have to steal you away for a minute. I need you to fill out some paperwork. Then you'll come right back." Jennifer leads Felecia from Kasey's desk to the human resources department.

Kasey still has the carnations in her hand. She looks down and reads the card to herself.

I saw your carnations dying the other day and thought these might bring your desk back to life.

Thinking of you,

Austin.

Blushing again, Kasey sits down in her chair. She has never received such a sweet, romantic gesture from a man. It renders her weak.

Jennifer walks back to Kasey's desk, and excitedly sits in the chair next to her. "Okay, the newbie's gone. Now you can tell me the truth. What's going on? Who's the boyfriend you couldn't tell one of your closest friends about?"

"Shut up. I don't have a man. It's nothing. Forget it." Austin seems sweet to Kasey, but he is not a romantic interest.

"I don't think it's nothing, by the way you're acting." Jennifer notices the card in Kasey's hand. She leans over and snatches it. After reading the card to herself, she rolls her eyes in amazement.

"Excuse me, this sounds like a whole lot of something. You have somebody, and you didn't tell me." Jennifer crosses her arms and looks at Kasey sternly.

"I don't have anyone, I swear. It's just this guy from the other day. He dropped off a package, and he was flirting with me."

"Well, it sounds like he's got a major crush on you. If he took the time to notice your plants were dying." Jennifer is impressed by Austin's attention to detail. She is interested to find out more about him. Kasey, on the other hand, is no longer paying attention to Jennifer. She looks down at her desk. Jennifer waves her hands in front of Kasey's face in an attempt to regain her attention. "Hello?! Oh my GOD, that's so cute, and not to mention thoughtful too."

Kasey looks up at her. "Yeah I guess. He left his card the other day, too." Kasey puts the carnations on her desk. She reaches over to open one of her desk drawers and takes out Austin's business card.

Jennifer's eyebrow rises. "And why haven't you called him yet? I'm sorry. You know I love you, but your love life has been in the dumps lately."

Jennifer loves her friend, and would love it if Kasey found someone to be close to. She only wants the best for her, and hopes she finds love one day. But as is often the case, Jennifer has been a bit too blunt. Kasey goes silent, showing her displeasure by way of body language.

"All I'm saying is, give him a call. What's the harm in having one dinner? If you don't like him, then don't go out with him anymore. At least give him one chance."

When Kasey was a young child, her father molested her repeatedly for years. Her mother often participated and would even hold her down. Desperate to keep a man, her mother did whatever it took to appease him, even if it meant harming Kasey in the process. Kasey was taken away from her parents at the age of nine. She has been alone since that day. The abuse she experienced has left her distrustful of people, especially men. She avoids relationships like a disease.

Processing Jennifer's reasoning, Kasey looks defeated. Jennifer is the closest thing she has to family. She always hears her out, even when she does not want to.

"It might be good for you. If nothing else, call him just to thank him for the flowers." Jennifer gives Kasey an endearing look.

"Okay, I will," Kasey agrees.

"Okay. Well, I have to get back to work. I'll see you later." Jennifer hands Kasey back Austin's business card. She gets up and heads back to her office.

Kasey stares at Austin's card. She decides to call him, but not now. She has to process her thoughts first. She puts the card in her purse for a later time.

After work, Kasey pulls into her driveway and turns off her car. She made it home with a couple of hours of daylight to spare, which is a rare occurrence.

Exhausted, she makes her way into her living room. The color pink ignites a deep passion in Kasey. Her entire house is pink-themed with pink furniture and black paint on the walls. She tosses her tote bag on the ground and flops onto the couch with her purse still on her arm. Her body sinks into the couch. Her head begins to throb from the stress of her workday. She massages her temples and begins to relax a bit. As she lays back on the couch to rest, she accidently knocks over her purse. The contents of her purse spill onto the floor. This further irritates her. She bends over to clean up her belongings. As she cleans up her belongings, she notices the business card with Austin's number on it. This helps her remember Jennifer's advice. She replaces her belongings into her purse, but keeps the card in her hand as she sits back on the couch. Now is the time. She decides to go for it. She picks up the phone next to the couch. She takes one last moment to think her decision through. With her composure in check, she dials Austin's number. After a few rings, a voice answers.

"Hello."

"Hi, it's Kasey." She hopes Austin cannot tell how nervous she is.

"I've been waiting on your call," Austin admits in a chipper voice.

Kasey relaxes. "I just wanted to call and thank you for the flowers. They were beautiful."

"You're welcome. I was thinking of you." Austin is confident when he talks to Kasey. This helps reel her in.

"Well, it's very thoughtful. I appreciate it."

"Well, you're welcome." Austin pauses. "I'm getting the feeling that thanking me was not the only reason why you called." He pauses for another moment. "I want to see you again."

Now Kasey pauses, as her guard continues to drop. "I guess that wouldn't hurt."

"Is Friday good?"

Kasey blushes. "Yeah, that's good. I'll see you then."

"I'll look forward to it." Austin means it. He cannot wait to see Kasey.

"Okay, bye." Kasey hangs up. She feels wrapped up in a fantasy world. This is the type of world she thought she would never allow herself to experience.

That Friday night, she sits in front of the vanity in her master bedroom. She gently strokes blush onto her cheeks. She uses every second before Austin arrives to put together the final touches. She is beautifully put together, from head to toe.

She stands up and walks over to a full length mirror. She smiles, knowing her looks are impeccable. She turns around to check out her backside. At that moment, the doorbell rings.

Kasey takes her makeup and puts it all back in its proper place on her vanity. Everything has to match in her home, and everything has an assigned place. She did not have control over what happened to her as a child, so she makes sure to control every detail that happens in her life as an adult. She looks in the full length mirror once more, for final confirmation. She feels confident and optimistic.

Before long, Kasey and Austin sit at a beautifully decorated table at an expensive, romantic restaurant. Kasey takes a bite of her salad. She looks up, and notices Austin admiring her every move.

"What?" Kasey covers her mouth while she continues to chew.

"You're so beautiful."

"And you're wonderful. I have to admit, I'm glad we did this."

"I hope we can continue." Austin reaches over the table and grabs Kasey's hand. "I have a surprise for you." Austin waves at the host, who picks up the phone from his podium and begins to dial.

"What's going on?" Kasey turns around, trying to figure out what the surprise could be. Three violinists walk up behind her. She quickly turns to face Austin.

"I just want this night to be perfect and never end. I just want something more with you. I think these guys can explain it better with this song." Austin signals, and the violinists begin playing. They play a beautiful love song. The sensual music causes the entire restaurant to stop and listen. Charmed, the women in the restaurant cannot take their eyes off of Austin. But Austin's eyes remain on Kasey.

"I'm speechless. No one has ever done anything like this for me before."

"Get used to it. My mom used to play the violin. I miss her music. Violins make such beautiful sounds." Austin gazes into her eyes.

The violinists continue to play soft serenades, as a few women whisper to their dates about how romantic the scene is. While most of the patrons turn their attention back to their meals, a few continue to stare at Kasey and Austin. "What's your mother's name?" Kasey is smitten. She wants to know everything about him now.

"Tracie. Tracie O'Neil. She passed away a long time ago." Austin pauses for a moment. "I just miss her, and I wanted to share some things with you that are very special to me." Austin begins to get emotional, as he always does when he talks about his mother.

Kasey puts her hand over her heart. Her eyes start to well up. Austin grabs her hand and gently kisses it. When Kasey looks into Austin's eyes, their bond is sealed.

The next morning, Kasey sits on Jennifer's bed while Jennifer sits in front of a vanity nearby, applying makeup. "It was amazing." Kasey falls back onto the bed.

"I can tell. You're acting like a little girl." Jennifer continues to apply her makeup.

"I can't help it." Beaming, Kasey twiddles her hair.

"So...tell me what happened." Jennifer turns around to give Kasey her full attention.

Just as Kasey is about to spill all the juicy details, Jennifer's son barges into the room. Brent is an energetic child who has trouble staying still. Although he is hyper, he has a sense of maturity. Growing up without a father, Brent has learned a lot on his own. This is evident in his expansive vocabulary, among other things. Having just returned from baseball practice, he is still wearing his baseball uniform. He was too anxious to see his mother to bother changing. Kasey and Jennifer turn to face him.

"Excuse me. I didn't know you had company. I'm sorry." Brent's eagerness turns into embarrassment.

"No, it's okay honey." Jennifer gets up and walks over to hug him.

Brent then walks over and hugs Kasey. "Hi, Kasey."

"How did practice go?" Kasey tickles Brent, who giggles loudly.

"It was awesome. I hit two deep in the outfield. It was incredible."

Jennifer sits back down at the vanity. "I'm so proud of you. When's your next game, sweetie?"

"It's next Saturday at three o'clock. I have to be there two hours early, so I can practice."

"Okay, calm down. You will be there early. Go clean up and get something to eat, so Kasey and I can finish talking." Jennifer kisses her son on the cheek.

"Okay. Bye, Kasey." Brent waves and leaves the room.

"Bye, sweetheart." Kasey waves back. Once he is out of the room, she turns back to Jennifer and laughs. "I swear he gets bigger every day."

"As often as I have to buy clothes for him, trust me I know. Okay now, finish what you were saying."

"Oh, where was I?" Kasey pauses. "Oh, yes. Well we had a really nice dinner. The whole night was magical." Her giddiness returns.

Listening to her friend's story, Jennifer becomes giddy, as well. She is excited to see a spark in Kasey's eyes.

"And a violinist played soft music," Kasey concludes. She smiles with pride.

"Oh my GOD, are you kidding me?" Kasey shakes her head no.

"How romantic! That was so impressive."

"I know. The night was perfect. He was just--- perfect." Kasey blushes yet again, thinking about all that might happen in her future with Austin.

"It looks like you got a winner." Kasey and Jennifer are both smiling from ear to ear. "Aren't you glad you took my advice?"

"Yeah." Kasey nods. Kasey and Austin's love seems to be destined to stand the test of time.

Love always comes by surprise. When love happens, you take it and run with it. When love happens, they say, follow your heart. But how can you when your heart is blinded? This is where the advice of friends can give us perspective. Friends can give us advice about love, family, and even other friends. We cherish this, because our friends mean us well. Although our friends mean us well, we must choose carefully which advice to listen to.

Kasey leans back on Jennifer's bed in a blissful state. The seed Austin planted has turned into a blossom of love.

Chapter Ten:

All Advice
Is Not Good Advice

Kasey is working on her computer, when Felecia walks up to her desk. "Hey, girlie. What are you doing tonight?" Felecia leans against her desk. Kasey looks up at her friend. "I haven't really thought about it."

"Come out with Jennifer and me. We're going to go out to eat and catch a flick. You have to come and have a girl's night. It'll be so much fun."

Kasey picks up a stack of sealed envelopes, and they walk down the hall towards the break room. "Are we going to sit up all night and talk about boys?" Kasey teases Felecia, drawing a laugh. "No, seriously, that sounds like fun. Count me in."

They enter the break room, where Jennifer is already at the refreshment table talking on her phone. Jennifer waves to them, while still continuing her conversation. Kasey walks over to the mailbox on the wall and starts to put sealed envelopes in their designated boxes. Felecia goes to the refreshment table and pours some coffee. After Jennifer finishes her phone call, she joins Felecia at the table. "What are you two doing?"

"I'm just trying to convince Kasey to come with us tonight."

Kasey finishes filling mailboxes and joins the conversation. "I said, I was all for it."

"Okay, then it's settled." They make their way out of the break room laughing. Their laughter is soon interrupted, when Jennifer notices a man standing at Kasey's desk. She points him out to Kasey. "Who is this at your desk?"

Kasey looks up, surprised. "It's Austin." She runs to Austin and leaps into his arms. She greets him with a warm hug and kiss. "Hi, baby. What are you doing here?"

Austin smiles. "I just wanted to surprise you."

"Well, you certainly did." Kasey bats her eyes.

"I feel like I know him from somewhere," Felecia whispers to Jennifer as they approach. Kasey eagerly motions for them to come closer.

"I want you guys to meet my boyfriend." Kasey hangs onto Austin's arm and smiles gleefully as she gazes up at him.

Felecia reaches out to shake Austin's hand. "You're Chase, right? It's been awhile. How have you been?"

Austin, Kasey, and Jennifer are all puzzled. Austin seems particularly alarmed.

"No, actually, it's Austin. It's nice to meet you." Austin reaches out to shake Felecia's hand.

"Felecia, it's nice to meet you." Felecia shakes Austin's hand. They exchange a chilling glare.

Austin reaches to shake Jennifer's hand next. "It's nice to meet you. I'm Austin."

Jennifer returns the handshake. "It's nice to meet you, too. I've heard so much about you."

Austin turns to Kasey and puts his arm around her waist. "I wanted to take you to dinner, love." He pulls her in close.

"That sounds great, but I had plans with the girls tonight." Kasey looks over at her co-workers, with disappointment in her eyes. She wants to keep her plans with her friends, but she also wants to nurture her budding relationship.

Austin grabs Kasey from behind and holds her firmly. "I hope you two lovely ladies don't mind me stealing Kasey away for the evening." Austin looks directly at Jennifer as he kisses Kasey on the cheek. Kasey smiles.

Jennifer and Felecia look at each other. "No, enjoy yourself. We'll do it some other time." Jennifer cannot shake the feeling that Austin was trying to steal Kasey away just so he could rub it in their faces. She got the creeps from the way Austin looked at her while kissing Kasey.

"Okay, it was nice meeting you ladies. Have a good day." Austin and Kasey walk off, hand in hand.

Jennifer looks over at Felecia, who suddenly looks paler. Felecia stands frozen in place. She is consumed by an overwhelming sense of confusion as she watches Austin walk away with Kasey. She knows Austin from somewhere; the sensation nags and eats away at her.

"Felecia. Hello? Girl, snap out of it." Jennifer gives Felecia a little shake to get her attention. "What's wrong with you?"

"I know him. I swear I know him."

Jennifer lowers her voice. "What are you talking about?"

"You didn't notice the way he looked at me when I called him Chase? I know him."

"His name is Austin. Maybe you're just thinking of someone else."

"Yeah...maybe you're right." Felecia shrugs.

Jennifer is certain Felecia is experiencing a case of mistaken identity. We come across people that remind us of other people on a daily basis. Some people just have the kind of friendly, familiar looking face that brings out a sense of nostalgia. Jennifer brushes off Felecia's suspicion as just a case of déjà vu. Despite her initial uneasiness about Austin's exaggerated display of affection, Jennifer has a great feeling about him. His charm is working on her, as it has done on many others. Jennifer advised Kasey to pursue a relationship with Austin...but sometimes all advice is not good advice.

Chapter Eleven:

It Is Not a Dream

Kasey stands on an exercise mat, in a yoga class with about ten other people. The instructor enters the room. She walks to the front of the class to set up. Kasey looks around the class, comparing herself with the other people in the room. She usually devotes most of her free time to the gym, but she has lost focus since her relationship with Austin began. This is her first workout in three months. Although her physique is still chiseled, her stamina has suffered greatly. After a few minutes, Kasey begins to sweat profusely.

After the class, Kasey heads straight for the locker room. Today, she decides to shower before leaving the gym. She usually waits to shower when she gets home, but today is a special occasion. Kasey and

Austin are celebrating six months together this evening. She decides to shower before leaving the gym, because their date is just a few short hours away. After showering, Kasey quickly puts on a spare set of gym clothes. She rushes out of the locker room with her cell phone in hand.

Before she leaves, Kasey walks up to the front desk to pay her monthly bill. She hands her credit card to the receptionist, who informs her that the machine is down. Unfortunately, her payment will have to be entered manually. Austin hates it when Kasey is late. Fearing the worse, Kasey's frustration begins to build. As she takes out her phone to kill some time by texting friends, a well-muscled gentleman walks up next to her at the desk. He looks at Kasey up and down, examining her alluring curves.

"How are you, Kasey?"

Kasey turns around to see Derrick, an acquaintance from the gym. Since meeting over a year ago, they have only bumped into each other occasionally. Their conversations had never gone beyond random chatter about health and fitness. "Fine. How have you been, Derrick? I haven't seen you in a couple of months."

"I've been out of town. Where are Jennifer and Felecia?" Kasey, Jennifer, and Felecia are inseparable. When you see one, usually the other two are not far behind.

Kasey laughs. She has become accustomed to people wondering where her partners in crime are. "Oh I came by myself today."

"I know this is a little forward. I've been meaning to ask you, but I never can get you alone. I'm glad you're alone. I've wanted to ask you something and it's a perfect time right now." Derrick pauses. Kasey gets nervous. She hopes Derrick does not put her in an awkward position. She is in love with Austin, and most importantly she is committed to their relationship.

"Felecia is so beautiful to me. I don't know how to approach her. I know this is random, but could you help me?" Derrick is uncharacteristically shy when it comes to Felecia, despite his outward virility.

The receptionist hangs up the phone and hands Kasey her credit card back. "Derrick, can you hang on one second?" Kasey finishes her transaction with the receptionist before continuing her conversation with Derrick. After signing the credit card receipt, she turns her attention back to Derrick. She ponders on Derrick's confession. She is relieved that she is not the object of his affection. However, she is still placed in an awkward position. She has not heard Felecia mention Derrick before. She does not even know if Felecia knows who he is. Honestly, she is not sure Felecia would ever be interested in a guy like Derrick. She decides that checking with her friend would be the safest and most respectful way to handle the situation.

"You know what, text me later. I'll see what I can do." Derrick smiles, and shows his gratitude with a hug.

Kasey heads for the front door. "Text me later. See ya."

Later that evening, Austin pulls into Kasey's driveway. He turns off the ignition. Before exiting his vehicle, he takes a moment to reflect. It is almost time for their Saturday night date. This date is particularly special as it is the celebration of their sixth-month anniversary. Austin pulls out a small ring box from his pocket. A lustrous engagement ring is revealed when Austin opens the box. His life could change for the better, if Kasey agrees to marry him. Austin is understandably nervous. Hopeful for a positive outcome, Austin gets out of his car. He carefully places the ring box back in his pocket. He takes a deep breath as he walks to Kasey's front door.

In the kitchen, Kasey opens the stove. The casserole she has prepared has baked to a crisp, golden brown. She carefully takes it out of the oven and puts it on her kitchen island to cool. The dining room is filled with flowers; which Kasey has received from Austin over the past couple of days. Flowers are his way of showing how much he truly cares. The lights are dimmed, and a bottle of champagne sits in a bucket of ice on the coffee table.

Kasey goes to the dining room to do some last minute checks. She does a quick scan of the entire area. Kasey's cell phone begins to vibrate on the kitchen counter. She does not notice it, because she is still in the dining room. Eventually, it vibrates off the edge of the counter. The cell phone crashes onto the floor, causing the battery to fly in one direction while the rest of the phone flies in another. Startled by the crashing sound, Kasey goes into the kitchen to find her phone in pieces. Annoyed, she picks it up and reassembles it. While the phone is rebooting, she walks back into the living room and puts it on the table next to her couch. The man of the hour is almost here. As the final touch, she goes to the stereo and puts on some mood music.

Kasey looks over at the clock sitting at the top of the entertainment center. It is fifteen minutes till seven; Austin should have been here by now. Just as her frustration begins to build, the doorbell rings.

Butterflies flutter in her stomach. On her way to open the door, she takes one last look in one of the many mirrors in her house. She opens the door to see the love of her life standing on the other side. She squeezes him tightly. "Hi honey."

Austin hugs Kasey with one hand. "I got something for you." He brings his other hand from behind his back, revealing a small bouquet of bright daisies.

"Aw, how sweet!" Kasey is overwhelmed with emotion as she takes the flowers. To her, flowers are the ultimate gift. All of Austin's attention makes Kasey feel like the luckiest woman in the world. Attention and adulation are all she has ever wanted from a man.

"I knew you would love them." Austin steps through the door and greets Kasey with a passionate kiss.

Kasey leads Austin into the dining room, where he looks around in amazement at the amount of effort and care she put into preparing for their evening. His heart warms at the sound of violins, which Kasey set up because she knows how much the sound of violins mean to him. She stands in the hallway, nervously awaiting his reaction.

Austin turns and walks toward Kasey. "Baby, you really outdid yourself." She smiles, relieved, as he holds her tightly. "I love everything you've done for me. I can't explain the way I feel."

Austin pulls Kasey's face in for a fervent kiss. His love for her is undeniable, and he wants her to feel it with their every embrace and kiss. He continues to gently kiss Kasey as he runs his hands down her backside. Kasey enjoys his touch. She squirms from the tingling sensation it gives her. Austin loves the fact that his touch makes her squirm. He slides his hands up her dress, exposing her underwear. Although she can barely stand the pleasure, Kasey gently moves his hands away. She is careful not to cast the impression that she is not interested in his advances. She just wants him to slow down for the moment. "Later." She softly kisses his nose to reassure him.

"Okay." Austin playfully rolls his eyes and follows her back into the dining room.

About twenty minutes later, they have almost completed the casserole Kasey prepared. Austin, appreciative of a meal which he greatly enjoyed, finishes his glass of champange in one sip. "Oh, I'm stuffed."

"You sure?" There's more if you want some."

Austin smiles and shakes his head. "I couldn't eat another bite."

"Well, I guess my job is done." Brimming with pride at having orchestrated a successful dinner, Kasey gets up from her seat. She takes their plates and goes into the kitchen to place them in the sink. She decides not to clean them right away, because she is eager to get back to her love.

Before she even gets to the sink, Austin gets up and follows her in. "Oh, you think your job is done?"

Kasey turns back toward Austin and smiles flirtatiously. Then she continues to walk into the kitchen. She puts the dishes in the sink and walks back into the dining room. Austin, who was hiding in a nook around the corner from the dining room entrance, appears and sweeps her off her feet. He cradles her in his arms, as a mother would her infant. Kasey smiles at Austin, awash in a sense of completion. In his arms, she feels protected and loved.

"Your job hasn't even started yet." Austin carries her into the living room. Kasey giggles as Austin playfully kisses her neck. He plops her on the couch, prepared to ravage her. Austin climbs on top of Kasey, slowly covering her neck with kisses. She is powerless to resist his urges, and that is how he likes it. His hands explore her body from head to toe. He is very good at what he does.

As her body continues to contort with pleasure, he slides his hands down her legs and spreads them apart.

As the heat between them continues to rise, Kasey's cell phone vibrates on the end table by the couch.

At first, Austin does not notice. When it vibrates again, he looks up in mild frustration. "Is that your phone?"

"It's probably no one." Kasey hastily pulls Austin in and kisses him. Her phone vibrates again, this time from a call.

Austin cannot tear his eyes away from the incessant vibrations coming from Kasey's phone. He pulls away from Kasey's kiss. He maintains his pleasant demeanor, despite his increasing discomfort. "Why don't you go upstairs and change…you know…into something." Austin strokes Kasey's long raven locks.

"Something more comfortable, right?" Kasey smiles.

"No---I was going to tell you to change into something that had a lot of nothing in it." Austin smiles seductively as he scoots closer to her on the couch.

"Okay. I'll be back." She stands up and walks out of the room.

Once she disappears, Austin's smile instantly fades. His anger and jealousy take over as he reaches for Kasey's phone. He scrolls through the missed calls, and sees Derrick's name. He has never heard Kasey ever mention anyone by the name of Derrick before. Austin immediately jumps to conclusions. He is hurt and enraged by the possibility Kasey could be cheating. He opens Kasey's text message from Derrick.

It reads: *I've been trying to call you. We need to talk.*

Austin looks up and shakes his head in disbelief. Sadness, anger, and shock overwhelm his thought process. His father robbed him of his mother, and his entire life has been overshadowed by the pain of having someone stolen from him. He views Kasey as something he controls, and the thought of losing control of her--even worse, *stolen from him*-- unleashes his inner rage.

Kasey returns, dressed to seduce. She twirls around playfully hoping to entice Austin. Oblivious to Austin's festering rage, Kasey leans against the wall.

She rubs her hands up and down her caramel legs. She wants to continue their evening upstairs in the bedroom. She motions for Austin to come to her.

Austin stares at Kasey's body. Her pink lingerie accentuates her brown skin. Austin gets up and walks to her. Kasey grins in anticipation. When Austin reaches her, she wraps her arms around his neck. She kisses his chin then his cheek. She slowly moves her lips to his ear, then whispers into it.

"I love you. I love you so much." Her sincerity could not be more obvious.

"Oh you love me?" Austin's expression is blank. His dry voice confuses Kasey.

"Of course I love you. You're everything I want." She leans back so she can look into his eyes.

"You know I love you…right?" Austin's eyebrow rises.

"Of course. And I love you too." Kasey looks uneasy.

"I would do anything for you. When I hear your voice, whatever I'm going through is instantly better. I only wanna hear your voice throughout the day." Austin pauses and looks deeply into Kasey's eyes. "I love talking to only you. Do you love talking to me?" Austin waits for Kasey to answer, but in his mind he is already convinced her answer will be a lie.

"I love talking to you, too." Kasey frowns uncertainly.

"You love talking to me, huh? Are you sure?" Austin's tone sharpens.

"What's going on? Is everything okay?"

"I don't know---I'm just trying to figure out if you like talking to me so much, why are you talking to some guy named Derrick?"

"What are you talking about?"

"You know I'm already really angry, but playing dumb only makes me angrier." Austin feels his body tense.

"Why are you getting angry? Derrick is just a friend. This is crazy."

"What did you just say? Did you just call me crazy?" He walks towards her. Flustered, Kasey begins to stammer through explanations, trying to calm him down. He leans his body against her, pinning her small frame against the wall. He grabs both of her arms. It is at this moment that Kasey becomes scared. She and Austin have never had a disagreement, let alone a fight. Her mind races as she tries to wriggle away.

"You need to calm down. You're overreacting. It's not what it looks like. I don't text other men." He keeps her arms pinned to the wall. Kasey tries to remain calm, not wanting Austin to see her panic.

"Oh, I'm overreacting...you wanna see overreacting?" Austin lets go of Kasey's arms and walks into the living room. He grabs Kasey's cell phone off the table. He begins to walk back to Kasey, but stops after a few steps. Blinded by hurt and rage as he remembers Derrick's name flashing on the screen, he throws the phone at Kasey. She ducks right before the phone strikes her in the head. Terrified, she stays crouched on the floor. She curls into a fetal position, shaking in fear and disbelief.

The loving, compassionate Austin she knew is now gone. In an instant, Austin has become his father, the man he despises the most. He walks over and stands above Kasey with menace in his eyes. He slowly bends down over Kasey, the same way his father used to. Kasey looks down, refusing to look at him--just as Austin's mother used to, during his father Steve's assaults.

Austin's gaze sends a chill up Kasey's spine as he decides that he has not made his point yet. With his left hand, he grabs her by the hair and jerks her head back in one quick motion. With his right hand, he squeezes her jaw and violently tilts her face upward. He wants her to look into his eyes. Controlling Kasey is essential to Austin's psyche; he has done it before, only with gentler methods. Times have changed.

"I'm overreacting? You're texting men, and probably *fucking* them too, but I'm overreacting. I think I'm acting pretty normal." Austin's right eye twitches. He has lost all touch with reality.

Kasey begins to cry softly. She pleads with Austin, explaining that her relationship with Derrick is strictly platonic. When he mocks her pleas, she begins to lose hope.

"I love you and you do this to me. Are you trying to make me look like a fool? Do I look stupid to you?" He looks into Kasey's eyes. He wants to see the fear. He waits for Kasey to answer; her silence angers him. He views it as open defiance.

He screams into her face. "You think I'm *stupid*."

Kasey shakes her head no. She begins to cry harder and more uncontrollably.

Austin, whose mind tends to play tricks on him in moments like this, begins to lose it. He grabs Kasey's throat, closing his grip as she struggles for air. As her air dwindles and her vision fades, Kasey begins to panic and struggle more desperately. She swipes at his hand as his grip continues to tighten. She scans the area, hoping for something to grab. Unfortunately, she cannot reach anything. Her consciousness begins to fade.

In a daring and final attempt, Kasey kicks her legs at Austin. As she swings her legs about, her knee catches Austin in the groin. Austin screams in agony as he releases his grip and falls on his back. "Fuck." He remains on the floor, immobilized from the pain.

Kasey runs out of the hallway and back into the kitchen. In survival mode now, she frantically searches one drawer after another for a knife. She empties every drawer onto the floor, feeling more desperate. Finally, she flings open a drawer and finds it filled with knives. A few of them spill onto the floor, nearly hitting her feet. She carelessly digs into the drawer and slices her right hand along one of the blades. "Dammit." Blood oozes from her right hand as she continues to search with her left. She finds a sizeable blade and turns around.

Her fear increasing with every step, Kasey creeps back into the dining room. The creaking floor increases her anxiety as she walks through the room. She stops in front of the hallway where Austin attacked her. She scans the area, hoping for something to grab. A noise makes Kasey stop dead in her tracks. It appears to come from the hallway. Fearful that

Austin could be there, Kasey slowly backs away from the hallway.

"Are you looking for me?"

Kasey wheels around to see Austin on her left, hiding in the same place he had hidden earlier. Kasey screams with fright at the sight of Austin, who stands in the corner calmly. She drops the knife, which clinks on the hardwood floor. Then she screams at Austin. "What's wrong with you?" Austin raises his eyebrow in confusion, which throws Kasey into a rage of her own. "Really? Are you kidding me? Get out." She points at the door.

"We had a little misunderstanding." Now that he has lost the upper hand, Austin's reaction is to try to defuse the situation and charm his way back to normalcy.

"Misunderstanding? You tried to fucking kill me. Get the fuck out,"

"Sometimes I just get out of control. I just lose track of what happens." Austin becomes emotional as he tries to explain his violent mood swings. "Please, baby…forgive me." Austin rushes over to Kasey and falls at her feet. He clenches her legs tightly.

Kasey is momentarily weakened. Her love for Austin pours out through the tears rolling down her face. She sobs uncontrollably. Her heart hurts. One moment, her future was bright and full of romance; a fiery romance. Now her relationship has turned into ashes.

"Please, baby. Forgive me." Austin grovels at her feet. He cries so loudly that it sounds artificial. "I'm sorry. Please, I need you." Austin squeezes her legs more tightly.

Feeling distraught, Kasey relents and drops to her knees. The bloody knife rests by her right side. The bleeding in her right hand is starting to slow, but her tears continue to flow. She looks down at Austin, who hangs his head low in shame. She glimpses at the hallway, which is in total disarray. She cautiously plots her next move.

"I love you. I---love you so much." Kasey seems frighteningly serious. Her voice is dry and emotionless. She raises Austin's head and gazes deeply into his eyes. Austin, now confused, looks at her hopefully.

"I want to be with you. You're everything I thought I ever wanted. Okay?" Kasey pauses momentarily; she always gets emotional while she looks into Austin's eyes. "But…no one and I mean *no one* puts their fucking hands on me." Kasey grabs the knife and quickly jabs Austin in the stomach.

Austin's face immediately contorts. He shrieks in agony. Kasey continues to kneel on the floor, still holding the bloody knife. She sneers at Austin. She enjoys watching him stumble around in pain. Hurting him felt almost *too* good. She continues to revel in his pain as she slowly rises to her feet. The tables have turned, and the power is hers now. Austin finally stumbles backward onto the dining room table, crashing to the floor with such force that he loses consciousness.

With Austin now helpless, it is time for Kasey to return to character. She has to step away from the part of herself that took pleasure in plunging the knife into Austin. She rushes to the phone to dial 911. She pulls herself together. Even though she very much acted in self-defense, she cannot show any sign that she enjoyed what she did.

At first, the altercation felt like a horrible dream. When Kasey examines the destruction in her home, it fully sinks in that this situation is really happening. It is not a dream.

Chapter Twelve:

She Can Run
but
She Cannot Hide

Jennifer sits at her desk in her office. She flips through the pages of a newspaper and takes a sip from her coffee. This is around the time of the morning when she meets with Kasey at the front desk to give her the day's agenda. She sneaks in some girl talk, as well. She leaves her coffee on her desk, picks up the agenda and exits her office. When she arrives at the receptionist's desk, someone other than Kasey is sitting there. Since joining the firm, Kasey has only missed one day of work; it was for jury duty.

"Where's Kasey?"

The temporary receptionist looks up at Jennifer. "I don't know. I'm filling in today. The regular girl is sick."

"Okay. Thanks." Jennifer walks back to her office and sits at her desk. She puts the phone on speaker and calls Kasey's number. The call goes straight to Kasey's voicemail. Jennifer ends the call, concerned. Kasey is obsessed with her cell phone, and it is always on. She picks up her phone again, this time not on speaker. She re-dials Kasey. It goes straight to voicemail again, so she leaves a message.

"Hey Kasey. I heard you were sick. I wanted to give you a call just to check on you. Let me know if you need anything." Jennifer pauses for a moment. "Call me. Feel better, sweetie."

Still damp from a hot shower, Kasey covers herself with a towel. She enters the bedroom. Her voicemail machine beeps from three new messages. She smiles, comforted, when she hears Jennifer's message. Then she plays the next one.

"Kasey---Kasey. Pick up the phone. I'm so sorry honey. Just talk to me please. Please." Austin's message ends. Kasey's peaceful expression fades. Despair sinks in as the third message plays.

"Pick up the phone. Kasey, we've got to talk. I love you so much. I was an idiot. I need you. Please pick up. I love you." Austin begins to cry and stumble through his words as the message continues. "I just got home. I'm alone. I need to talk to you. Things got out of control, but we can work on it. Please— Please." The voicemail ends.

Kasey goes to her closet and slowly chooses an outfit for the day. Her right hand is still bandaged from the night before. She unwraps her towel and lets it slowly glide off her body, revealing the abrasions and bruises from Austin's assault. Her back and hands hurt as she struggles to put her clothes on.

Once dressed, Kasey walks into her bathroom to glance in the mirror. She gradually raises her head, afraid of what she might discover. The woman who loves to look in the mirror has not yet mustered the courage to do so. Looking at the terrible bruising and scars around her neck, Kasey feels immeasurable shame. She does not want to believe the bruises are real, but touching her tender wounds confirms the reality of the situation. She was abused last night.

Following a long, hard look in the mirror, angry tears begin to fill Kasey's eyes. Examining the results of Austin's brutality enrages her. Kasey's anger boils to a dangerous level. She slams the medicine cabinet shut, shattering the glass from its mirror. She steps on some glass as she storms out of the bathroom. Her anger numbs her ability to feel any pain from the glass.

Back at the office, Felecia walks into Jennifer's office with a stack of papers in her hands. Completely focused on her cell phone, Jennifer is unaware of her entry. Felecia sees an opportunity to get a rise out of her normally alert friend. Felecia playfully drops the stack of papers on Jennifer's desk to startle her. Jennifer jumps in her chair and gasps. Upon noticing Felicia, she chuckles. "Holy shit, you scared the hell out of me."

"I'm sorry. I had to. I'm sorry." Felecia shares a laugh with her friend, then resumes a professional demeanor. "Here's the briefing for next week."

"Thanks." Jennifer stands up and sifts through the paperwork.

"Hey, have you heard from Kasey? We were supposed to go to lunch today, but I haven't seen her."

"Well, she's out sick today. There's a temp in for her. I tried to call her twice, but I haven't gotten a response."

Jennifer's concern is evident, so Felicia decides to comfort her. "Well, she's probably okay. People get sick."

"Yeah, maybe you're right." Jennifer lightens up a bit. "I was gonna swing by her house after work and check on her. You wanna come?"

"Definitely." Felecia was thinking of checking on Kasey herself.

Inside Kasey's house, trash bags have begun to proliferate. Half-empty food containers litter different parts of the living room, which is a complete mess. Normally obsessed with the order of things in her home, Kasey sleeps on the couch in the midst of the disarray.

There is a knock at Kasey's front door, loud enough that she is startled from her sleep. A partially eaten container of melted ice cream splatters onto the living room carpet, making a huge stain on the carpet. As the knock at the door continues, Kasey unwillingly sits up. She rubs her eyes and looks around. She looks with disinterest at the ice cream spill, which would normally send her into a fit of anger.

Jennifer and Felecia wait patiently outside. Felecia holds a bowl of soup. The front door opens just enough for a sliver of Kasey to appear. Jennifer immediately reaches out to hug Kasey. After seeing Kasey's disheveled appearance, she pulls back with a grin. "Hey...eeeew. What happened to you?" Unaware of Kasey's fragile state, Jennifer is just engaging in a bit of their usual teasing. Kasey walks away without uttering a word, leaving the front door wide open. Jennifer and Felecia walk in. Jennifer closes the door behind them.

Kasey walks into the living room. She steps over the spilled ice cream and flops back onto the couch. She stretches out on her back and puts a pillow over her face. Felecia and Jennifer are flabbergasted at the mess in her home.

"How are you feeling, sweetie? I brought you some soup." Felecia walks over to an end table to put the soup down. Used tissue and food wrappers cover the end table. Felecia scrunches her face up and changes her mind. "On second thought, I'll just go to the kitchen and get something to put this in." She takes the soup to the kitchen. "And maybe I'll find something to clean some of this mess up."

Jennifer sits down next to Kasey on the couch. "What's wrong, girl? This place looks a mess." Kasey offers no response. Jennifer shouts to get her attention. "Kasey!" When she still does not reply, Jennifer reaches over and yanks the pillow off of her. Her eyes widen when she sees the bruises on Kasey's neck.

"What happened to your neck?" Not waiting for an answer, she immediately sets off to look for Felecia.

Kasey's eyes well up with tears. She begins to cry uncontrollably. Jennifer calls out to Felecia, who rushes back into the living room. Then Jennifer turns back to Kasey, now feeling even more alarmed. "What in the hell happened to your neck?" She calls again for Felecia, unaware that she has already returned.

"What's going on?" Felecia walks around the couch to see what the commotion is about. Now face to face with Kasey, she observes the bruises for herself. She covers her mouth with her hand, gasping from shock.

Jennifer grabs Kasey's arm. Kasey's arms are still tender with bruises. She jerks her arm away. "Ow."

Gently, Jennifer pulls up Kasey's sleeves. Seeing more bruising, she recoils in horror. Felecia, trying to restore calm, walks over to Kasey. She kneels down directly in front of Kasey. "Who did this to you? Tell me what happened. You can tell me." She is nearly whispering.

"Please tell us," Jennifer pleads.

Grief-stricken tears run down Kasey's face. "I don't know. It all happened so fast." There is a moment of silence as she gathers herself to speak. Felecia and Jennifer lean in closely.

"We were having such a romantic night. Then he just snapped. He just went into a rage. I've never been so scared in my life."

"That son of a bitch," Jennifer utters out loud. Austin's violence outrages her. Worst of all, she was the one who encouraged Kasey to go out with Austin. Though she is not at all to blame for the situation, she feels a considerable amount of guilt.

"Wait…who did this?" Felecia does not want to believe Austin is the person who put such bruises on her friend's body.

"Was it Austin?" Jennifer already knows the answer, but asks anyway.

Kasey bows her head and nods.

"That motherfucker." Felecia joins them on the couch.

Kasey sits up and rustles her hands through her hair. "I don't know what to do. He won't stop calling. I'm going crazy." She feels sullen and desperate.

Jennifer and Felecia lean in and hug her firmly. If one of them hurts, they all do. Jennifer strokes Kasey's disheveled hair. "Don't worry about anything. Everything's going to be okay."

Felicia nods. "You always have us. That's what we're here for. When you don't know what to do, we're here to help. Come with us."

Thinking about it, Kasey knows she is better off where Austin cannot locate her. "I don't know what I would do without you two." The three friends share another embrace.

Sometime later, Jennifer and Felecia have packed Jennifer's trunk with some of Kasey's belongings. Kasey walks out the front door holding more of her belongings in a bag. Felecia walks over to her and takes her bag. They get into Jennifer's car and pull out of the driveway. This is the first time Kasey has felt peace in days. Hopefully under Jennifer's roof, she can get away from the drama and return to some state of normalcy.

Just as the car disappears into the darkness, Austin appears from behind a bush next to Kasey's house.

He watched them pack Kasey's belongings. He watched them talk in the living room. He saw the entire thing. In his eyes, they are trying to take Kasey away from him. He will not stand for it. He stares into the darkness as Jennifer's car disappears down the street. He is more determined than ever to get Kasey back. Kasey is his one, eternal love. She can run, but she cannot hide.

Chapter Thirteen:

The Power of The Mind

Kasey sits on the couch next to Jennifer's son, Brent. He snuggles under a blanket next to her while she holds the remote. She has been staying with Jennifer for the past couple of days. For now, she seems to have returned close to her normal self; she has even laughed a few times. Being around Brent has helped tremendously.

"Okay...what do you wanna watch?"

"Something scary." Brent shows a big, toothy grin.

Kasey laughs. "I don't think so." Jennifer would kill her.

"You can say that again." Jennifer enters the living room holding a bowl of popcorn. "There's no way I'm letting you watch a scary movie."

Brent scowls. "Aw, *mom*."

"I don't wanna hear it. It's not happening."

Jennifer hands Brent the bowl of popcorn as she sits next to him. Kasey hands her the remote. Jennifer flips through the channels until she finds an animated children's movie. Kasey laughs to herself. Despite all she is going through, she finds peace in her time with Jennifer and Brent. She watches Brent eat his popcorn and giggle innocently at the movie. His sprightly presence has a calming effect on her. She rests her head on a pillow on the couch. Before she knows it, she has drifted off to sleep.

As Kasey coasts into a deep sleep, her surroundings become unfamiliar. She is unaware of her unfamiliar surroundings, because she is still asleep. Instead of the couch she fell asleep on, now she is lying on a bed that seems to be made for a child. The bed is so small; she has to curl into a fetal position to fit on it. The room is poorly kept, with weathered walls and rundown furniture. Unbeknownst to her, Kasey is in Austin's childhood bed. Unfortunately, this is the same room where Austin's mother was murdered.

A thunderous knock at the bedroom door awakens her. Kasey jumps out of her sleep. Discovering her strange surroundings, Kasey freezes. She scans the room, trembling. Initially, the knocking sound came from the bedroom door. After scanning the room, she realizes that the knocking is not coming from the bedroom door anymore—it is now coming from behind the closet door. Kasey's eyes widen as she notices the closet door shaking. It looks as if it might come off the hinges.

Kasey rises to her feet and makes her way to the bedroom door. She keeps her eyes on the rumbling closet door as she walks to the bedroom door. Looking for an escape, Kasey rushes out into the hallway. A powerful white light fills the entire hallway. While shielding her eyes, Kasey walks down the hallway. Even though every instinct tells her to run away, she continues down the hallway. As she walks into the blinding light, it swallows her whole. The powerful light leads to a white, empty room without windows or furniture. Suddenly the room begins to spin.

As the room spins faster, and faster, Kasey becomes dizzy. She covers her eyes with her hands, as nausea takes over. After a few moments, the spinning suddenly stops. Within an instance, things almost feel deceptively normal. After the spinning stops, Kasey slowly removes her hands from her eyes. The fear in her heart fizzles away as her eyes open. She stands alone in the room, confused. As she turns to walk away, she unexpectedly bumps into someone. It is Austin, who was standing directly behind her. As Kasey screams helplessly, Austin looks at her with dead, maniacal eyes.

"Going somewhere?"

Kasey wakes up screaming.

She looks around to find herself in Jennifer's living room. She sits up and runs her hands through her hair. Her nightmare leaves her shaken. She cautiously makes her way to her feet. The heavy bags under her eyes continue to darken with each passing day. Kasey rubs her eyes as she walks out of the living room.

"Good morning," Jennifer greets Kasey with a smile. She and Brent are at the table eating breakfast. Kasey waves, without looking up.

Jennifer watches Kasey drag herself across the kitchen. "Did you have a rough night?"

Kasey nods as she sits down. She rests her head on the table, and tries to fall back asleep.

Jennifer taps Brent on the hand. "Baby, go take your cereal in the living room." He takes his bowl of cereal and mindfully walks out of the kitchen.

Jennifer lightly touches Kasey's arm. "What's wrong?" "I just had a bad dream." Kasey still rests her head on the table.

"Was it about *him*?"

Kasey nods silently.

"Do you want to talk about it?"

Kasey shakes her head.

"Why don't you go out and have some fun? It might make you feel better."

Kasey drops her head and begins to cry quietly.

"Sweetie, I'm sorry. I didn't mean to push you or…"

Kasey interrupts. "It's not that---I don't know. I just feel like I'm going crazy. Like, I see him everywhere. I feel followed. I'm losing it." Kasey wipes tears from her cheeks.

Brent runs into the kitchen. "Mom, come on. Practice starts soon." He is fully dressed for practice, and he cannot contain his excitement. He runs out of the kitchen to get his baseball bag.

Kasey smiles and stands up. She wipes away the rest of her tears. "We'll talk when you get home."

"Are you sure?"

"Yeah, I'll be here when you get back. I'm just going to work out and take a bath. Hopefully that will relieve some stress and make me feel better." Kasey offers a smile.

"Okay, well practice won't be long. Maybe we could go out to lunch and talk then?" Jennifer stands up.

"Okay, I probably need that." Kasey stands up and hugs Jennifer goodbye.

Feeling slightly better about leaving Kasey by herself for a bit, Jennifer chugs the rest of her coffee. She places the mug in the sink and heads out with Brent. Kasey washes the dishes and goes up to her room to change. She is looking forward to a workout; working out has always been an excellent way to relieve her stress. When she works out, she can tune out the world and escape. She walks down the hallway to Jennifer's in-home gym, and gets on the treadmill.

After running for a bit, Kasey gets on the squat machine. Her back faces the door. A creaking sound in the floor startles her. She looks over her shoulder. When she sees nothing, she continues her workout.

After working out for another thirty minutes or so, she heads for the bathroom to clean off. She sits on the side of the tub, holding her iPod in her right hand. Her body still bears scars from her altercation with Austin. She places her iPod on the edge of the tub. As the hot water runs, she gets undressed. A dark silhouette moves past the open doorway. Just as the dark silhouette disappears, Kasey turns around. She leans over and pushes the door shut.

Once she is settled into her steaming bath, Kasey places her headphones in her ears. Then, Kasey puts her iPod back down on the edge of the tub. A lace blindfold over her eyes is the finishing touch on her soothing getaway. She wiggles along with the music as she sings happily. She is as relaxed as she has been for a while.

Suddenly, the door creaks open. She thinks she hears a noise. She quickly snatches her blindfold off her eyes and her headphones out of her ears. She is all alone, yet the door sits wide open, along with the window. She is pretty sure both were closed when she got into the tub. The curtains ripple gently, though it is not windy outside. She scans the room again and sees no one. Deciding that her mind is playing tricks on her, she tosses her iPod on the floor and rises to her feet. She wraps herself with a towel. Then, she carefully steps out of the tub and walks over to the mirror.

After wiping the steam off the mirror, Kasey dries herself off. She puts on a sexy pair of boy shorts and a matching bra. She grabs her brush and starts to brush the tangles out of her wet hair. She tries styling her hair, which proves problematic. "Ugh...my hair just refuses to act right," she huffs out loud. A familiar voice responds from the background.

"I think it looks beautiful."

Kasey freezes. She dreads turning around to see who she knows is there. She turns around to find the bathroom door closed, and Austin standing in front of it casually.

"What are you doing here?" Kasey is quivering from head to toe.

"I told you nothing could keep us apart. You can't hide from me." Austin takes a step towards her. Kasey takes a cautious step back.

"I've missed you so much." Austin takes another step forward.

"No..." Kasey takes another step back.

"I've missed you." Austin takes another step. "The way you used to smile at me. Your kisses. Your body." Austin grins gaily as he looks at Kasey's exposed skin.

Reeling from shock, Kasey looks all over the room for a way out of the situation. Austin takes a last, quick step forward. They are face to face. He gently strokes her wet hair. Kasey flinches, repulsed by his touch. Austin savors touching Kasey's skin again, the way he used to. For a moment, he thinks things are back to normal. He leans in close to her.

"I love you so much. I want to work things out. I can't be without you." He gently kisses her forehead. Kasey pulls away, but Austin pulls her in closer to his body. Feeling cornered, Kasey gives in to Austin's advances. Kasey breathes deeply, then wraps her arms around his neck.

"I have to admit something. I've wanted to see you for some time now." Kasey smiles warmly.

"Really?" This stuns Austin.

Kasey nods. "Yeah, I did. I've been waiting to." Kasey hesitates. She sensually gazes into Austin's eyes, the way she used to look at him when things were great. Time slows down.

Euphoric, Austin squeezes Kasey and strokes her cheek. "So what have you been waiting to do?"

"I've been waiting to give you something." Kasey leans in and gives Austin a long, delicate kiss. Kasey leans in close to Austin, her mouth close to his ear. All he wants is for her to say they can work it out and that he has her back.

"This." With a swift thrust, Kasey kicks Austin in the groin.

Austin collapses to his knees, moaning. Kasey scampers past him in the direction of the door. She almost makes it. Just as she gets within arm's reach of the door, Austin reaches from the floor and grabs

Kasey by her leg. Kasey falls violently, slamming her right cheek onto the cold tile floor. She looks back at Austin, who is still on the floor in pain. Kasey tries to regain her footing, but she is dizzy from hitting her head. As she makes it to her knees, Austin clutches her ankle. She drops back down to her belly. She glances back, petrified. Austin maintains a firm grip, now having grabbed both of her ankles. She kicks at him frantically, shouting at him to stop. Eventually, he loses his grip on one of her legs.

"Let---me--*go*!" She kicks hard with her free leg.

Austin makes it to his feet and drags her by the leg he still controls. "Get back here."

Kasey begins to feel desperate. As Austin drags Kasey across the tile floor, Kasey tries to pull away from him. If Austin regains control of both of her legs, the situation will end badly. Kasey hopelessly tries to grab the door. Her chance of escaping dissipates as Austin continues to drag her further into the bathroom. She brings her left leg back to her chest for one powerful last-ditch kick. Kasey kicks Austin squarely in the nose. The impact knocks him backward into the tub. The back of his head suffers the worst of the fall, slamming into the tile wall. As his rage builds, blood oozes from his nose and head.

He lightly smears some of the blood across his face when he touches his nose.

Kasey jumps to her feet and darts towards the door. She turns the handle and swings the door open. As she sets foot in the hallway, Austin grabs her by the hair and jerks her backward. "Where the hell do you think you're going?" As her screams intensify, he grabs her by the waist. He picks her up effortlessly and slams her to the floor. Her head hits the edge of the sink on the way down, knocking her out cold. Her body lands face down, as a pool of blood slowly begins to spread around her head.

Austin walks over slowly. His nose, chin, and mouth are covered in his own blood. He bends down and carefully strokes Kasey's mangled, bloody hair. As he strokes, he exposes her battered face. Blood saturates Austin's hand as he continues to stroke Kasey's hair obsessively. "You look so beautiful." He leans in and softly kisses her cheek. Then he scoops her and sits with his back against the tub, cradling her like a newborn. As he draws her head into his chest, panic rushes over him as he realizes what he has done.

"I didn't mean to hurt you." Austin begins to weep. "What did I do? Oh my GOD, what did I do?"

His crying turns hysterical as he presses his face into hers.

"Why did you have to do this? Be so difficult, huh? I never meant to hurt you. This is all your fault. Why did you fight me? This didn't have to happen. I thought we were going to be together forever. I always thought you were going to be Mrs. Chase O'Neil. It's me---Chase. I love you. Why would you run from me? I thought you loved me." Austin lowers his head as he breaks down once more. He looks back at the tub full of water, then back at Kasey. His heart fills with regret. He has injured her badly, and there is only one way out of the situation. He has to end her suffering. He decides to put Kasey in her final resting place.

Austin slowly rises to his knees, then his feet. He still cradles his beloved in his arms. He turns and faces the tub, and kisses Kasey's lips. The kiss is long, passionate and heartfelt, albeit not returned. He loves her deeply, even though, he has hurt her profoundly. But now it is time to let go of her completely.

Austin slowly lowers Kasey's lifeless body into the water. As he watches somberly, she sinks to the bottom like a stone.

Blood from Kasey's head wound seeps through the water like a virus. As she slips away, he sheds a final tear. Then he turns and walks away, as quietly as he entered.

After a few moments, bubbles surface at the top of the water. Kasey's eyes flash open and dart around. She is submerged in water, bloody water that muffles her attempts to scream. Panic ensues when Kasey cannot sit up right away. She flails for a moment, until her hands find the edge of the tub. She sits up, splashing water all over the bathroom floor.

Kasey looks around, terrified. There is no sign of the violent struggle that took place moments before. No broken glass, no blood soaked floors. She touches her head, and finds neither a wound nor blood. She looks down at the water; the blood has disappeared from there, as well. She rubs her face trying to clear her head. While sitting in the tub, she draws her knees toward her chest. "What...huh?" Completely befuddled, she places her chin upon her knees. She slowly rocks back and forth, as she tries to make sense of what just happened.

Later that evening, Kasey sits on Jennifer's bed. "I'm telling you, I'm not crazy."

Jennifer replies in a soothing tone. "I didn't say you were crazy."

"It was so *real*. He was attacking me. It wasn't a dream." Kasey shakes her head. "No way."

"I know...it was crazy and so realistic, it shook you to your core, but it was a dream."

"And you know what really got me, is that he kept saying his name was Chase."

"Chase?" Jennifer laughs, as Kasey gazes out the window. "Maybe it was some mix-up. You know you never quite remember everything about your dreams...things always get distorted." Kasey throws up her hands in frustration, as Jennifer continues in a soothing tone.

"Look I believe you. I'm on your side. All I'm saying is maybe that incident with Austin affected you more than you think. I just think you're seriously traumatized. Now hear me out, okay?" She pauses. "Maybe you need to go talk to someone about this."

"Oh no. I don't think so."

"Come on, Kasey. You are really stressed. You know you're bothered by all of this. You need to talk to someone other than me."

"If I go to a shrink, that means I'm admitting I'm crazy." She points an index finger at Jennifer. "I am *not crazy*." She gets up and storms out of the room.

Jennifer watches in sadness. Even though Kasey fled to Jennifer's house, she cannot escape Austin. He resides in her mind.

Raging silently in her bedroom, Kasey ponders her dream. The most memorable part of the dream was Austin referring to himself as Chase. There has to be a deeper meaning behind this. The mind is a magnificent thing. It has the ability to make you see things that are not actually there, and if you believe in them, they can seem incredibly real. That is the power of the mind.

Chapter Fourteen:

The Stare She Could Never Forget

Paying only cursory attention to the rules of the road, Kasey tears through the streets of downtown Seattle. She pulls to a screeching halt in a parking lot outside of the library. She hops out with her purse over her shoulder. She single-mindedly makes her way to a computer, though she is almost afraid to turn it on. She is in search of the truth, but does not know if she can handle what she will find. She does an internet search for 'unpredictable emotional disorders.' She is not a doctor, but she feels certain that Austin is suffering from some kind of mental illness.

A link about borderline personality disorder catches her attention. She clicks on the link, and skims through the symptoms of this disorder. The description fits Austin to a tee.

Kasey sits back in her chair to process her new discovery. Then she leans forward and begins another search, this time for Austin O'Neil. The search turns up nothing of interest for numerous pages. She is about to throw in the towel when she clicks on one last link, to an old news article.

Tracie O'Neil, mother of two, found dead at the age of 31. Father Steve O'Neil pleads guilty to the beating death of wife, Tracie and son, Austin.

The news hits Kasey like a ton of bricks. She remembers her first date with Austin, when he talked about his mother at their romantic dinner. He had said her name was Tracie.

The article continues: *The only survivor was eleven-year-old son Chase O'Neil.* The picture of Chase O'Neil looks exactly like the man she knows as Austin O'Neil.

The man that she knows as Austin is really Chase. The visions in her dreams were correct. She begins another search, this time for Chase O'Neil.

Chase O'Neil was a suspect in the 2006 kidnapping and murder of seventeen-year-old girl,

Leann Wilson. Charges were never filed, due to lack of evidence.

Kasey prints off the news articles so she can keep it as evidence. Devastated, Kasey runs to her car and peels out of the driveway.

Two hours later, she is sitting in a coffee shop with sunglasses on. Gripped by paranoia, she looks over her shoulder constantly. People around her are talking to each other and working on their computers. In her mind, they are all staring at her. Her hair is unkempt, and she has not worn makeup in a week.

Jennifer and Felecia rush in. Once they spot her, they hustle over to her table. Felicia sits next to her. "Are you alright?"

Jennifer grabs a chair from a different table and sits on the other side of Kasey. "I got your calls. You scared me to death."

Kasey reaches in her purse and pulls out a small stack of papers. She looks at Jennifer and Felecia as she slowly unfolds them. She gets emotional as she places the papers down on the table. Felecia picks them up first. After reading for a few moments, her face goes slack. The information on the paper causes her to reflect on a distant memory.

About eight years earlier, Felecia was staring out the window of her house. She was eleven at the time.

She was looking into the eyes of a young boy, sitting in the back of an ambulance as two body bags were transported to the curb. "Oh my GOD."

Jennifer and Kasey both turn to her. "What?"

Felecia shakes her head. "I knew it."

"Wait...hold on." Jennifer snatches the papers out of Felecia's hands. "What am I reading here? Is this true?"

Kasey takes off her sunglasses and puts them on the table.

Felecia leans forward. "Remember when you introduced him to us and I called him Chase? Remember?"

Jennifer and Kasey begin to connect the dots. Kasey begins to hyperventilate. She repeats her friend's utterance. "Oh my GOD."

Felecia taps her finger against the news articles. "Now we can't question whether it's true or not. It's right there, in black and white." She *knew* his name was Chase; her suspicions had continued to nag her since the day Kasey introduced them. If she had been more insistent, maybe her friend would not be going through this pain.

Jennifer falls back against her seat. "I'm speechless...I don't know what to say."

Kasey turns livid. "I can't do this anymore. I can't live like this anymore. I'm having delusions; I'm going crazy. What am I supposed to do? Wait until he kills me?" She shakes her head vigorously. "No, not me." A couple of heads turn in the coffee shop.

Jennifer lowers her voice to a soothing tone. "Now, wait a minute. I know all this is difficult. You had a violent experience happen to you, and you found out the man you love has been lying to you. This is all very traumatic, I know. Felecia and I are here for you, and we will do whatever we can to help. But this...this is all too much."

Kasey turns and snaps at her friend. "*What is too much?*"

"All I'm saying is you're sounding crazy. You've got to think clearly. I really think talking to a therapist will help. This has completely altered your personality and train of thought. I know this is horrible and traumatizing, but you can't lose yourself in the process. I mean, we'll go with you if you want us to. I will." Felecia, wracked with guilt, nods in agreement.

Kasey takes a moment to think. "You're right. I need to do something to fix what I'm going through. I'm not going to lose myself." Kasey puts on her sunglasses and takes her wallet from her purse. She fishes out a picture of the man she now knows is Chase. In the photo, they are hugging each other tightly. Things seemed wonderful. Kasey's eyes begin to well up and tears run down her cheeks.

Jennifer begins to cry. Felecia, tears running down her face as well, squeezes Kasey around the shoulders.

Kasey pulls back and steadies herself. "Will you guys trust whatever decision I make?"

"Of course." Jennifer wipes her tears away.

"Don't ever doubt it." Felecia smiles.

Kasey violently tears up the photo. "I've made my decision." She stands, still holding the remnants of the photo along with her purse.

"What are you going to do?" Jennifer tries to make eye contact with Kasey, who's still looking at the torn up photo in her palm. She dumps the pieces on the table. They scatter, some falling to the floor.

"You'll find out soon. Trust me." Kasey walks toward the door, smirking.

Felecia calls after her friend. "*Kasey!*" When Kasey stops and turns, Felecia can only think of one thing to say. "Take care of yourself." Kasey nods.

Jennifer chimes in, trying to sound hopeful. "See you soon?"

Kasey pauses to reflect, then points an assertive finger in her friends' direction.

"Count on it."

As Kasey walks out the door, Felecia and Jennifer embrace.

In most relationships, whether healthy or unhealthy, two people become enjoined as one. It usually happens without you even noticing. But only in an unhealthy relationship is your vanishing identity so apparent. Many girls lose themselves in the chaos of a turbulent relationship. Little did Kasey know, her turbulent relationship would bring her identity to pass. All because of Felecia's confirmed suspicions, and the stare she could never forget.

Chapter Fifteen:

The Reincarnation of Kasey Laine

Chase lies on his bed, holding his cell phone. His heart aches for Kasey. He opens his phone and sends her a text message. He waits anxiously for her response. In his mind, Kasey still wants to be with him.

Kasey sits on a park bench, watching the sun go down. The colors are even more beautiful than the park that surrounds her. She soaks it all in, as the breeze gently rustles her polished hair. She closes her eyes. She takes a deep breath as she tilts her head back.

Her cell phone buzzes. A text from Chase flashes on the screen.

Frazzled, she puts her phone face down on the bench and crosses her arms. She is not sure what to do next. The colorful sunset calms her rattled nerves. Despite the way she feels inside, she cannot resist the urge to respond to Chase's text. She dials his number. As the phone starts to ring, she loses her nerve and hangs up.

Kasey gazes into the sky as the sun sets. Suddenly, her mind begins to replay the events from that fateful night with Chase. She remembers how tight his grip around her neck felt. She flashes back to being dragged across the room. All at once, everything is put back into perspective. She picks up the phone and redials Chase's number.

"Hello."

"It's me," she nearly whispers.

"Kasey?" Chase is overjoyed. He has waited for months to hear her voice.

"Yes."

"I'm so glad to hear from you. I've wanted to talk to you so bad."

"I think we need to talk, but not now. At least not over the phone." Her voice cracks.

"I miss seeing your face. I miss your voice. I miss you...I just miss you."

"Is tomorrow night good for you?" Against her will, Kasey blushes.

"Of course---I want to see you and work this all out. I've been miserable." This time his voice cracks. Kasey can tell he is now in tears.

"Yeah, I know what you mean. I've been miserable too. This has really been hard for me." The truth is, a small part of her does miss him.

"It's been hard for me too. I'm so sorry. All I want to do is show you how sorry I am." His voice is hindered by more tears.

Kasey assumes a more upbeat tone. "Well, we can talk about everything tomorrow night. Figure it all out."

"Okay, till tomorrow. I love you. I want to make this work. I promise you. I'll do anything to make it work." He prays for Kasey to hear the remorse in his voice.

Kasey hesitates. "I love you too. I'll see you tomorrow." She hangs up.

Relieved, Chase puts his phone down and stretches out on his bed. This day could not have ended more perfectly; Kasey is coming back home to him. He closes his eyes and falls into a deep sleep. At exactly six in the morning, his alarm goes off. It takes him a couple of tries to silence the alarm. Still drowsy,

Chase stretches in his bed. Once dressed, Chase heads to work. It is Friday, he has got a date with Kasey, and he could not be happier.

At the warehouse, Jason picks up a box. It is too heavy for him, but he picks it up anyway. Chase enters the warehouse with pep in his step. He finds Jason struggling to maintain his grip on the box. On a typical day, he would simply laugh, but today he jogs over to help. "Whoa, whoa." He places his hands under two of the corners and helps Jason manage the weight. Once the box is stabilized, he laughs. "You look like you're struggling, man."

"Oh, you noticed," Jason responds with a smirk. They laugh together as they walk the box over to another stack of boxes. They lower it to the ground carefully.

"Thanks man," Jason huffs.

"No problem."

Jason leans on the stack of boxes. "What's wrong with you, man?" He breathes heavily.

"What do you mean?"

"I mean, you. You seem a little too happy today. '*You look like you're struggling.*'" Jason mimics Chase. "What's up with that? You're never that helpful. You would watch me fall on my ass any other day."

Chase smiles. "Well, things are going pretty good for me right now."

"That means..." Jason wrinkles his brow. Yesterday Chase was miserable; today he seems ecstatic.

"It's just that Kasey is coming over tonight." Just the thought of her brightens his day.

"Oh, I know what *that* means." Jason makes a lewd gesture.

"Shut up man. It's just I finally got her to talk to me. I'm feeling good right now. I want this to work. She's right for me."

"Well I hope it works, man. A little word of advice, test the waters...you know. You messed up, so just be prepared to have it thrown in your face constantly. Not once, not twice either. I mean like all the time; like ten times a day. I'm serious, too. That's what women do. You mess up once, and they'll bring that shit up every day till the day you die. Hell, they'll bring that shit up on your deathbed." Jason's tone turns silly. "Your heart monitor is beeping away and your ass is in a fucking coma. I promise you, she'll be right at your bedside nagging your ass about the time you fucked up twenty years ago. Watch, I'm not lying. Listen to me man. Bitchin' 101. Read it sometime." He is laughing now, trying to lighten the mood, but he is genuinely concerned for his friend. He does not want Chase to have unrealistic expectations. He and Kasey are not going to magically go back to the way they were, even if they both want it that way.

Chase waves a hand in dismissal. "I don't care about that, man. I just want her back. I will have to deal with all that just for her to come home. I'm gonna see her tonight."

"You alright?"

"Yeah." Chase shrugs.

"Well don't worry, everything will work out."

"I hope so too---for her sake."

"I mean I'm just saying I'm not giving up. I'd do anything to be with her. Steal, lie, kill...anything."

Jason laughs uneasily. He breathes a sigh of relief when their boss struts into the warehouse. He gruffly hands them clipboards with their day's routes. Jason comically mimics him after his exit, drawing laughs from Chase. His taunts always lighten the mood.

"Alright, check ya later." Jason heads out to begin his route.

"Alright."

On his way out, Jason pauses. He has a bad feeling about Chase's demeanor. His last comment about Kasey was especially unnerving.

Later that evening, Kasey prepares for her date with Chase. She puts the finishing touches on her makeup. After smoothing down some frizzy strands of hair, Kasey walks over to the full-length mirror in her bedroom. She turns from side to side, checking the views on her perfectly fitted dress. She walks to her bedroom door and reaches for a duffel bag she has packed. She drags it out of the room and down the hall, scraping it along the hardwood floor as she goes. The duffel bag is filled to its capacity. She struggles the entire way down the hall.

Meanwhile, Chase prepares for Kasey's arrival. He can barely control his nerves as he walks into his living room. He places two champagne glasses on the table. A bottle of champagne sits in a bucket of ice on the table. He pops the cork, producing a bubbly stream. After he fills the two glasses with champagne, he places the bottle back into the bucket of ice. There is a knock at the door.

Chase walks to the door, overjoyed, and lets Kasey in. Kasey is in full seduction mode, and turns on the charm immediately. In hopes of arousing Chase immediately, Kasey seductively walks past him. Chase can barely contain his urge to ravage her, but he knows he must control himself. In order to win

Kasey back, he needs to be patient, and on his best behavior.

Midway through dinner, Chase picks up a glass of champagne. "Should we toast?"

"To what?" Kasey tilts her head and smiles, as she flutters her eyelashes.

"Us being together again. This is special." Chase starts to raise his glass.

"Why don't we save the toast and get to what's really important?" Kasey giggles, her eyes focuses on Chase.

"And what's important to you?"

Kasey chugs the rest of her champagne before she answers Chase's question. Feeling playful, she plucks Chase's glass and chugs it as well. Chase has never seen her drink this way before; she seems loosened up. His anticipation builds.

"This is what matters: I love you, Chase." Still holding both glasses, she drapes her arms around his shoulders and hugs him tightly. Chase hugs her around the waist. They kiss passionately.

Later that evening, Chase sleeps soundly in his bed after a night of intimacy with Kasey. While Chase sleeps, Kasey sits across from him in a chair. She is barely visible because of the darkness in the room. She slowly rocks back and forth in the chair as she continues to watch Chase sleep. A baseball bat rests in her lap.

As she watches him sleep, there is no trace of love in her facial expression. She watches him like a bird of prey. She repeatedly taps the bat in her hand as she rocks back and forth in the chair. Convinced he is sound asleep; Kasey makes her move. She stands up and walks to the edge of the bed. Boldly, she turns on the lamp next to Chase. Her black, lifeless eyes now visible. In one sharp movement, Kasey raises the bat above her head and brings it down hard onto the side of Chase's head.

Chase goes from sound asleep to knocked out cold. A stream of blood runs from a gash above his hairline. She chuckles as she admires her work. Then, she quietly strolls over to turn off the light. The games have only just begun.

Chase wakes up at the dining room table. He sits slumped in a chair with blood running down his face. He slowly shakes his head, as pain flares from various parts of his body. His vision is blurred, but he can see a silhouette across from him. His groans turn to screams, as he realizes he is handcuffed to the chair.

"You might as well give up, because there's no use. Those cuffs aren't coming off." Kasey laughs cruelly.

"Kasey?"

"Uh huh." She chuckles, mocking his fear and confusion.

"What's going on?"

"Don't you know? We're working things out. Isn't this what you wanted?"

Feelings of pain and betrayal momentarily increase his strength. He screams again, in anger this time. He tries to jump up out of his cuffs. The handcuffs will not budge. He slumps back into his chair, defeated.

"Are you done? I think it's best if you calm down." Kasey waits. "Now if you listen and are a good boy, it'll be over quickly. But if you give me a hard time, I swear to GOD I'll make you suffer." Kasey gets up and walks over to him.

Chase hears her footsteps coming closer, then behind his chair. His chair is jerked around to face the silhouette which taunts him. He feels a soft kiss on his lips. As his vision begins to clear, he recognizes Kasey's face--but it is not the face he remembers. This face is cold, devoid of emotion. Chase looks over at the dining room table, where a razor-sharp hunting knife sits. He begins to panic.

"What are you doing? What are you going to do with that?"

Kasey glances at the knife and lets out a short, cynical laugh. She looks Chase in the eyes and strokes his hair. "Don't worry. We haven't gotten to that part yet." She smiles and walks out of the room.

While Kasey is away, Chase frantically looks around the room. He tries to wriggle out of the handcuffs, but they will not budge. He hears a scraping sound. Kasey appears in the doorway, dragging a heavy duffel bag. She sets it down and wipes her forehead. "Whew, now that's a heavy bag," she says affably. She unzips the bag. Chase begins to hyperventilate.

Kasey pulls out the contents of the bag: rope, then hedge trimmers, then pliers, and finally duct tape. She twirls each one playfully as she pulls them out and sets them down.

"What's that for?" Chase stutters his words, his eyes never leaving the bag's contents.

"Being a man, you like to get straight to the point." Kasey pauses to savor the anguish in Chase's eyes. She has been waiting for this moment. "But you see, I'm a woman and I'm into foreplay. I brought these along to help stimulate my mood. And since you kind of suck at foreplay, I thought I'd teach you a thing or two." Kasey grabs the pliers. She also pulls out a small stack of papers from her duffel bag. She brings both the pliers and papers over and sits in a chair next to him. She lightly runs the pliers through his hair.

"You're fucking crazy." Chase jerks his head away from the pliers.

Kasey doubles over with laughter. "I'm crazy. *I'm* crazy. Well, you must know the signs. Did your therapist teach you that? I'm crazy...okay, I'll be crazy then." Kasey shrugs. "Maybe you're right, but at least I'm not a liar. Yeah, I'm definitely not a liar. You got that area covered, don't you?"

"What are you talking about?"

"Do you really want to keep playing dumb, Chase?"

Chase's freezes.

"I'll ask you again. Do you want to keep playing dumb, Chase? Is there really even any point anymore? Your game is up. I mean really, I called you Chase hours ago--right before I fucked you. But you were too stupid to notice. It's over."

"Look, let's talk about this rationally." Chase keeps his voice steady as he tries to divert her attention from his hands, which he is still trying to wriggle from the cuffs.

"Rationally? You wanna talk rationally. Did you talk rationally to LeAnn?"

Chase falls silent.

"Oh yeah, I know about LeAnn and your family, and your fake identity. I know everything. I don't care what the papers say; I know you hurt that poor girl. I *know* it, you sick son of a bitch. And you know what the worst part is? You insult my intelligence by trying to carry on this lie---like I'm not going to find out." Kasey's voice rises, along with her rage. In one quick motion, she grabs the knife from the table and puts it to Chase's neck. "You really thought you were smarter than me, you spineless prick?" Kasey pushes the knife into his skin, drawing a thin line of blood. She screams directly into his face. "*Look at me.*"

Chase turns to Kasey and searches her lifeless eyes.

"I'm going to give you a chance to make it right. Do you want to make it right?" Once Chase nods, Kasey continues calmly. "Tell the truth. Tell the truth for once. I don't even know you. Everything was a lie." Kasey's voice quivers with the last sentence.

Chase breaks down into sobs. Minutes later, he is crying softly and shaking his head. His exaggerated sobs perplex her. She watches him closely, desperately waiting for a response. He finally lifts his head to speak. "I didn't want him to go. I wanted him to stay with me. I was alone and scared." He is looking through her, with tears still in his eyes.

"Austin, don't go.' I kept saying it." Chase bows his head again, visualizing the day that changed him forever. He recounts to her a memory he had never before discussed.

Eleven-year-old Chase sits in the closet with his brother, Austin, who is twelve. The door is slightly ajar, and through the opening Austin is watching their father, Steve. Steve is viciously attacking their mother, Tracie. Austin looks back at his frail younger brother. He reaches out to take his hand. "Everything will be okay. I need you to listen to me very carefully. Okay?" Chase is already afraid, but he is even more scared by how hard Austin is squeezing his hand. His face is salty from crying, which he has been doing since his parents' arguing began to escalate over a day ago.

"Okay, when I tell you to, I want you to run and find help. Anywhere. You hear me? Go get help, can you do that?" Chase nods. Austin hugs him as if he knows it will be the last time.

Steve sits on top of Tracie, choking her with both hands. He does not see that Austin has quietly made his way out of the closet, and has picked up a bottle from the end table.

Austin shatters the bottle over Steve's head. As Steve struggles to regain his balance, Austin turns to the closet. "Go---now."

Chase darts from the closet and runs out of the bedroom in a flash. He runs all the way to the front lawn, where he begins screaming for help.

Chase opens his eyes and looks at Kasey. He sits in the chair with his head down by his chest. His wrists are bloody from struggling against the handcuffs. He trembles from exhaustion. Kasey stands over him with her arms crossed. Unfortunately for Chase, his sob story has fallen on deaf ears.

"And LeAnn?"

While crying silently, Chase keeps his head down.

Kasey screams his name to get his attention. "What happened to LeAnn?" Her patience is running thin. She desperately wants answers so she resolves to keep her cool.

"I did it." His voice is barely audible.

"What?" Kasey leans in closer.

"I did it. Isn't that what you want to hear? Yes, I did it." Chase looks up, ashamed.

Kasey rolls her eyes. "Wow."

"I didn't mean to. I swear...I didn't mean to."

"Oh, and what did you mean to do?"

Chase laughs. "You think life is so simple. Well, it isn't. Sometimes things just happen and you're thrown into a situation. Then suddenly, you have to make a split-second decision. Then over time, you discover that split-second decision was the wrong decision. But now you're stuck, and can't take it back."

"So what happened?"

Chase closes his eyes. These are memories he had long ago buried. "I was driving down this highway, and I saw this skinny, sexy brunette walking along the side of the road. She needed a ride, so I pulled over."

LeAnn Wilson walks alongside a seemingly deserted highway on the outskirts of Seattle. Rebelling against her family's values, she left home about a year ago. She has not looked back since. She has no friends or possessions, and she does not mind. She has adapted well to the transient lifestyle, because her beauty gets her from place to place. She was last dropped off about an hour ago, and has been walking since then.

A rundown car approaches in the distance, heading in the same direction LeAnn is walking. LeAnn hears it coming and turns around, signaling for the driver to stop. She puckers her lips and arches her back slightly, perking up her bosom. Chase likes what he sees, and pulls to a stop.

LeAnn leans on his open window provocatively, turning on the charm.

Chase glances first at her chest, then her face. "You need a ride?"

LeAnn smiles and bites the corner of her lip. "Sure." She gets in and closes the door. They quickly pull away.

"So, where are you heading?"

"Anywhere." LeAnn flicks her hair.

"Really?" Chase chuckles.

"Yeah, I don't have much family, so I'm just going wherever life takes me."

"Sounds adventurous." Chase looks into his rearview mirror. As he continues to drive, he passes a sign indicating a rest area is near.

"Oh, can you do me a favor and stop at that rest stop?"

"Sure."

They pull into the rest stop. LeAnn gets out and walks towards the bathroom. She freshens up for a few minutes, while Chase begins to get antsy. He turns on the radio, hoping it will help relax his nerves; he has never picked up a woman in this type of situation before.

LeAnn returns to the car and sits down. The second LeAnn settles in the car, Chase leans in and kisses her. The parking lot is deserted. They roughly transition to the back seat and start yanking each other's clothes off.

Later, Chase sleeps soundly in the back seat while LeAnn is wide awake. She crawls over him, careful not to rouse him. She positions herself in the front seat. She reaches into his pocket and locates his wallet. She takes out all of the money and stuffs it in her bra. She eases out of the car, with her purse and shoes in hand. She leaves the door wide open.

Just as she thinks she has made her getaway, Chase's eyes open. He looks around to find his car door open and his wallet on his chest devoid of cash. He sees LeAnn sneaking off into the dark. He immediately hops out of the car.

"Hey!"

LeAnn turns around to see Chase running toward her, gaining ground quickly. She hustles away. The money she stole spills onto the ground. Several paces in front of her is a curb that appears to border a wooded area. She is certain Chase will lose sight of her in the deep woods. Sadly, the curb borders on the edge of a deep embankment. She runs past the curb, through the thin barrier of trees, and right over the edge. She tumbles all the way to the bottom, hitting her head several times on the way down. Her fall ends when she hits a huge rock, with her head absorbing most of the landing.

Chase arrives to the edge of the embankment and looks down. He sees LeAnn at the bottom, unconscious and bleeding from the head. He makes his way down carefully, almost losing his footing several times. He believes LeAnn is dead. He feels trapped. He looks around, checking for witnesses, and notices a large, bloodstained rock. His mind races through possible outcomes, most of which involve him being blamed for her death. He decides he needs to guarantee her death. Besides, she had just stolen money from him.

He calmly approaches the rock. Before picking it up, he scans the area for people. The rock is very heavy. As he carries it over to LeAnn's body, she begins to stir. He does not panic; vengeance and self-preservation are the only things on his mind.

LeAnn's eyes widen in terror as she realizes Chase's intentions. She struggles to move, but can only twitch. She tries to scream, but her voice lacks sound. Chase grunts as he raises the rock above his head and slams it into her face. He slams it again and again, each time harder than the last. He turns, *covered in her blood, and checks again for witnesses one last time. He looks down at her body, feeling cold inside.*

Chase sits in the chair, more exhausted than before. "I didn't want this to happen, but I didn't have a choice." In his mind, LeAnn had robbed him and therefore deserved her fate.

Kasey, blown away, looms over him. "Are you kidding me? You didn't have a choice? What about getting her some help? Call an ambulance, you heartless bastard. Are you that cold that those options were out of the question? I see why you took on the identity of your dead brother now. You're a cold-blooded killer. Well, you're not going to get away with it anymore."

"It was too late. I was already going to be blamed for her death. I did what was necessary."

Kasey paces back and forth. She can barely process everything she has just heard. She continues to pace until she comes to a decision. "So there's nothing left to say. What's done is done." She turns and walks away. When she reaches the front door, she pauses. She is briefly overcome by a change of heart. She loved him once. But she came here on a mission.

"You know, there is something that I feel is necessary." Smiling, Kasey turns around to face him.

She walks over to the dining room table and picks up the knife. Kasey firmly clinches the knife as she marches towards Chase.

Chase begs for his life between screams of agony. He continues to scream as his life ebbs away. Kasey enjoys taking his life. In exacting her vengeance, she has discovered a new side of herself.

It is time to begin the reincarnation of Kasey Laine.

Chapter Sixteen:

The Hunt for KL Begins

C hase's apartment manager stands at his front door, nervously jangling his key ring. Several police officers are standing behind him. They had received numerous calls about Chase's apartment, referencing screaming and violent-sounding commotion. They announce themselves repeatedly, until the decision is made to breach the door.

Once inside, they fan out across the apartment. The officer who first happens onto the living room stops in his tracks. He gasps. He will never forget what he sees.

Chase's lifeless body slumps to the side, still handcuffed to the chair. The words "For LeAnn" are engraved deep into his chest. His body is riddled with stab wounds, all deep enough to draw blood but none deep enough to kill on their own. He bled out slowly, suffering to his last breath. The hunting knife sits lodged in his thigh; wrapped around the handle is a blood-saturated handkerchief, with the initials K and L written in pink lipstick.

Across the street, Kasey sits in her car with the engine running. She smirks, imagining the discovery of Chase's body. Kasey slowly drives off when all of the officers enter Chase's apartment.

Later that day, there is a knock at Jennifer's front door. She opens it to find two detectives waiting to speak with her. They tell her of Chase's murder, and inquire as to Kasey's whereabouts. She has not seen Kasey since their meeting at the coffee shop a few days ago, and she had been unaware of Chase's fate. She calmly explains that she has no idea where Kasey is. The detectives show Jennifer an evidence bag. Inside of the bag, is the blood soaked handkerchief. When Jennifer sees the initials K and L on the handkerchief, she panics inside. But her training as an attorney allows her to maintain her composure, even in the most stressful situations. In solidarity with her friend, she reveals nothing. The situation plays out similarly when the same two detectives visit Felecia.

Felecia's loyalty resides with Kasey. She does not reveal a single detail.

After the investigators leave, Jennifer sits in her living room. She burns a candle, hoping the soothing scent will take the edge off of her worrying. She looks out the window and sees the mail truck pull away. She walks to her mailbox. Inside it is a letter, with no return address. It has the initials "KL" written across the top, and a kiss in pink lipstick. She glances around quickly. Certain the coast is clear; she rushes back inside to sit on the sofa. Her heart pounds, as she opens the letter.

Jennifer,

By the time this reaches you, I'll be long gone. Due to the current circumstances, I think it's best to start a new life. Most people choose their own pathetic lives, meaningless dead-end jobs and relationships. Those people will never be worth shit. Simply born to take up space, and eventually leave the world just as unnoticeably as they came in. But for a lucky few, life is already chosen. Preordained. Destined. I am one of those lucky few. I have a purpose beyond the natural realm of this world. Whether it is for the best or the worst, the girl you once knew is no more. I can no longer run from my destiny. I must embrace it. Till we meet again.

Kasey Laine "KL"

While still holding the letter Jennifer closes her eyes. Even though she feels relieved to hear from Kasey, she is grief-stricken. Instantly, she recalls the visit from the detectives. She opens her eyes to glance at one of the detectives' cards on her coffee table. Jennifer has always been like a mother to Kasey; right or wrong, she knows what she has to do. She places the letter back in the envelope, and holds the envelope over the candle. Tears well up in her eyes as she watches it burn.

At the same time as the letter burns, Kasey walks down a scorching Arizona highway. Heat waves ripple the air. She dresses in a skin-tight leather outfit, her exposed skin glistening in the sunlight. Her makeup, as usual, is flawless. Her lips are pink, and her eyes are black. Her eyes sparkle behind her sunglasses.

In the horizon, a local bank becomes visible. She licks her lips, and lifts one eyebrow. She needs insurance for her life on the road, and this is the first step. She reaches under her jacket with both hands, and pulls out two sleek handguns. She looks over her shoulder and to both sides of the road; the coast is clear. She walks towards the bank with one goal in mind. Here is her opportunity to become the legend she is destined to be. Her transformation is complete.

Back in Seattle, the lead investigator watches the forensics team continue to search for clues in Chase's apartment. The only solid piece of evidence he has is the bloody handkerchief with the letters K and L. He holds this firmly, believing it will eventually lead to the killer.

The hunt for "KL" begins.

ABOUT THE AUTHOR

Dionndra Reneé is a talented new author who resides around the outskirts of Atlanta Georgia. Dionndra earned a Bachelor's degree in Criminal Justice and Forensic Science. She spends most of her time reading, writing, and taking long walks. Dionndra also spent close to a year volunteering at various Battered Women Shelters. During this time she witnessed first hand the long-term psychological and emotional trauma various women experience. It is here she received her inspiration to write her novel "Kasey Laine" which is the first of a five part series.

If you would like to contact or follow her at Twitter: @thekaseylaine, Instagram: kaseylainebook, Facebook: kaseylainebook, Email: kaseylainebook@yahoo.com, Manchuestate.com

Made in the USA
Coppell, TX
29 January 2021

49153426R00104